A gut-wrenching tale of a coal-mining community's bitter-most failings and one Polish family's glorious rising. *40 Patchtown* is evocative, haunting, told with page-turning momentum, and reveals an insider's understanding of the societal complexities that keep miners returning to the earth's dark underbelly. Damian Dressick, a talented and thoughtful writer, is the freshest voice to come out of Appalachia since Wiley Cash arrived on the literary scene.

—Karen Spears Zacharias, author of *Mother of Rain*

40 Patchtown reads like a cross between E.L. Doctorow's monumental novel *Billy Bathgate* and Breece Pancake's deathless story 'Hollow'—it's a work of fully imagined historical fiction that endows its characters with incandescent life, told in the unmistakable language of the early twentieth century coalfields. It pulls the neat trick of feeling bound to a highly specific time and place while simultaneously giving the impression of classic timelessness. As fine a first novel as one could hope for.

—Pinckney Benedict, author of *Miracle Boy and Other Stories*

40 PATCHTOWN

A NOVEL

DAMIAN DRESSICK

APPALACHIAN WRITING SERIES

BOTTOM DOG PRESS
HURON, OHIO

ISBN: 978-1-947504-196
Bottom Dog Press, Inc.
PO Box 425, Huron, OH 44839
Lsmithdog@aol.com
http://smithdocs.net

CREDITS:
General Editor: Larry Smith
Cover & Layout Design: Susanna Sharp-Schwacke
Front Cover Art and Photo on Page 2: Eureka Mine No. 37,
Windber Pennsylvania,
Coal Culture Project, Indiana University Library

Acknowledgements are on page 186.

*The author would like to thank
the Blue Mountain Center
for its generous support.*

That which is crooked can not be made straight:
Those which are wanting can not be numbered

— Ecclesiastes

But what is the strength of a boy!

— *Iliad*, Book XI

For
Alex and Jessie & Henry and Maggie

ONE

I can smell the bony fires blowing up the ridge from Eureka 40. The sulfur smoke drifts over the powerhouse, the driftmouth and across the railyard, tops the frame houses, wafts through McKluskey's stubble pasture and slides up into the bare trees, where it mixes with the cigarette smoke and corn whiskey stink coming off my brother Buzzy's pea coat— which is two sizes too big for me.

Little Mikey and me, we're keeping a watch. We're laying stock still. Our legs wrapped tight and our shoulders held low, our fingers is fixed fast to the fat high limb of the big silver maple jutting out of the woods off to the side of McKluskey's barn. Behind us, on the ground, in a tight cluster of oaks, my brother Buzzy—and Stash and Baldy, friends of his from down Eureka 37—stand waiting. It's been near twenty minutes since the mine whistle let loose the shift. Looking through the woods, cross the far pasture, I can already see a thin sliver of moon hanging low above McKluskey's barn.

My elbows ache fierce and I'm getting distracted, watching the breeze catch hold of my breath and push it up through the smooth, bare branches when Mikey digs his fingers into my arm.

"Look, Chet," Mikey cups a whisper into my ear. "Them damn scabs is coming up the hill!"

At first I don't see 'em, but when the scabs get over the next rise and start through the pasture, I can make out the light from their carbide lamps. I count two, then three, and I'm glad Buzzy brought his baseball bat. Mikey drops a rock to signal the fellas below us and I watch their shadows move forward in the darkness. I tighten my grip across the sharp-edged rock I snatched up down in the Paint Creek shallows.

But I ain't gonna hit nothing from here, so I slip the rock back in my pocket, and branch by branch, Mikey and me, we climb down outta the maple. At the last limb we let go and drop down into a thick pile of soggy leaves. Buzzy pulls me up by the hand and wraps his arm around my shoulder. He nods to me and Mikey. Stash and Baldy hold up their sticks and slap them into their hands. We get tight up against the trees and wait. I share a tree trunk with Buzzy. The dark brown bark is rough right flush up against my cheek, but I ain't gonna kick none about that. Buzzy sticks his head out every couple of seconds, keeping his eyes peeled for them scabs.

But in the end, it don't matter, cause them scabs coming up the rise is singing. A little quiet, maybe, but singing for sure. Some damn Eye-tailyan song that I can't make out quite. I poke my head out for a peek. When them Eye-ties draw even with the stand of oaks, I can see clear that there's really four of them. The one out front looks to be my age, fourteen, and the fat one in the middle with the cigarette, is maybe seventeen like Buzzy. The other two look grown. The one in front is thick-chested and limping a little. The scab trailing up the rear is tall, but real thin, like he ain't ate good for a while.

Buzzy takes a deep breath and steps out from behind the oak tree. I pop out on the other side. Buzzy pulls back his arm and heaves his rock. The piece of fieldstone whizzes right towards the chest of the scab with the limp.

Even through the heavy leather pit vest, Buzzy's rock must thud good and hard, cause the scab doubles over like and the rock plops to the ground. The scabs start yelling some kind of shit in the Eye-tailyan and one of the other scabs grabs the one that got hit by the crook of his arm and pulls him back up to standing. Then them Eye-ties start running like all hell.

Watching them scabs, Buzzy starts to yelling. His voice loud and deep, he's cursing them scabs out fierce. He calls them scabs "stinkin dagos" and "sunsabitches" as they dash by.

"Try and take *my* job, younz scabs better run," Buzzy shouts.

Them Eye-ties are going full-tilt when I let my rock fly. I take aim at the scab closest to the trees, but I don't hit nothing. Buzzy looks over at me sharp and quick. I wanna tell him I done my best, but I can see it ain't gonna make no difference to him. Either I hit the scab or I didn't—end of god damn story.

Scrambling into the woods, them Eye-tie scabs is dropping lunch pails, headlamps, blasting caps, the whole shooting match, making back for the showerhouse where they come from. Waving hickory switches, we're after 'em like dogs on a rabbit. They're cursing and we're heaving chunks of rock and yelling for them not to be scabbing on us.

Halfway down the ridge the scabs divide up and Mikey and Stash and me follow the kid, the limper and the old man through the woods along the edge of the pasture. Out the corner of my eye, I see Buzzy waving his bat while him and Baldy chase deeper into the woods after the tall scab.

Letting my switch drop to my side as I run in the twilight, I use my hand to keep the fast coming branches from smacking me cross my gob. I catch up to Mikey and Stash real easy cause I'm the fastest runner in all of 40 Patchtown.

When I get even with them, Mikey and Stash is whooping and hollering for them scabs to keep running. "Back ta Itlee, ya dagos!" After we been running a time, I can see Mikey and Stash are getting tired. Maybe losing their wind a bit. But I catch a flash of one of the scabs headed over the hill back towards McKluskey's farmhouse. I give a whoop and take off full of vinegar for the top of the rise—leaving Mikey and Stash to catch up with me as best they can.

When I get to the top of the hill, I rake my eyes cross the fields from the farmhouse down towards the tipple. But I don't see nothing. I turn back to look for Mikey and Stash. But the big chested scab must have been hiding hisself behind one of them oaks or locust trees, cause when I turn around for a second gander at the fields, he's standing there starring at me.

I raise up my switch and he eyes me curious. He says some shit in dago and starts walking towards me like he's just wanting to ask where they keep the lamp oil stocked in the pick-me store. I start whipping my switch around a bit, just to show him I mean business. But he keeps closing on me anyhow and I'm getting spooked and start shouting for Stash and Mikey.

The scab don't pay no mind till he hears Stash yelling back to me through the trees. Then he's in front of me quick and I realize for the first time just how much bigger the scab is than me. I know I'm small for fourteen, but you'd think I could do more than just look him right in the middle of his scab chest. Worrying I won't get no chance to get in a shot, I tighten my grip on the switch and wind up to take a poke. But the scab catches me by the wrist. I'm hollering blue murder and thanks to Christ, Stash and Mikey are both hollering back.

The scab looks back over my shoulder, and before I can say so much as boo, he lets me have one across the kisser. The punch puts me right on the ground and when I look up that scab's off through the woods back in the direction of the 40 driftmouth. Breathing hard, I rub my cheek and I can feel the smear of blood on my hand fore I even look. Mostly, I'm just in shock, like. I been in my share of scraps like all patchtown boys, but I never knowed anything could happen so fast as that scab's punch landing on me.

Stash and Mikey come crashing through the bushes at the top of the hill. Mikey's saying "Christ Almighty, Chester! Ya alright?" I'm nodding and then Stash is picking me up off the ground and putting my switch back into my hand.

I tell them that the scabs split up and I come face to face with the toughest one. Stash is laughing and says we should find Buzzy and Baldy and head back to 40 Patchtown.

When we find Buzzy, him and Baldy got the long-legged scab cornered down in McKluskey's drainage ditch. Baldy's on one side of the ditch and Buzzy's on the other. Every time the scab tries to climb out, they give him a whack on the hands.

"There's one scab gettin more than he bargained for," Stash says.

We're watching Baldy rap the Eye-tie a good one on his wrist when he tries to grip the straggly clusters of roots hanging down into the ditch. Mikey and me, we nod and the three of us push forward for a closer look.

The scab's splashing round in a foot or two of water and his hands is getting to look pretty well whacked apart, all scraped and bleeding. We're all yelling at the scab, telling him he's in deep. Stash and me start picking up little rocks and whipping 'em at the scab, catching him in his chest and his legs. He's putting his hands up and cursing us in dago.

Not one to take a cursing out from no scab, Buzzy jumps right down into that ditch. He's swinging the bat round, and the scab's ducking and bobbing and looking to bolt. But the scab, he can't get away cause the ditch is high on the sides and where the water comes down, it's steep and slick.

Scab oughtta know, we catch him he's due for a beat down. It's only fair. Ain't none of us been on strike six months starving so sunsabitches can come into Windber, Pennsylvania and earn four dollars a day scabbing Eurkea 40 Patchtown mine.

"Stand still and take yer medicine or you'll catch it worse," Buzzy tells him.

But the scab don't listen nohow and charges on Buzzy. Splashing through the water, he's reaching out like to grab Buzzy by his throat. But I ain't scared for Buzzy, cause he's plenty tough and got muscles like an ox from shoveling coal into them two-tonners on the B seam since he was younger than me. Besides, he's taller than our pa was 'fore he got killed down in them West Virginia mines.

"See how much ya can load with a broken arm, ya scabbin bastard!"

Buzzy swings on the scab like he's going hard for a fastball down Delaney Field. The bat's a blur, and I can hear it cut the air with a *whiiiff* and then there's a sound like a brick hitting a watermelon.

The scab's standing there all still, and Buzzy pulls the bat away from his ear. None of us are saying nothing. Buzzy lets the bat drop to his leg. The scab stands there for a second like he's froze, and we look at each other face to face round in a circle and there's a stillness, a calm like—like time can't go forward at all.

Then the scab crashes down into the dark water and it's like everyone can move again. Baldy says, "Jee Suss Christ." And Stash is squinting and looking at the body floating in the drainage and he says, "Jesus Christ is right."

"Is he dead?" Mikey asks.

"Buzzy," I says. "We better get outta here."

Buzzy shakes his head and shoves the bat in the water a couple of times trying to wash off the blood. He says, "My brother's right. Let's go."

We get clear of that drainage ditch right away and head back through the woods towards 40. We don't need telling, but Buzzy says we gotta keep our traps shut about the scab.

"It's a bad business," Stash says.

Buzzy nods and pulls a plug of tobacco from his britches. He bites off a corner and passes it round. When it comes to me, I gnaw a piece off and work the bitter plug back into my cheek. When everybody has some, Buzzy puts it back in his pocket and we start hoofing down the reddog toward the lights of the 40 Hotel.

Two

Our house is on Second Street of 40 Patchtown. We're to the front porch 'fore Buzzy notices my face is all swolled and cut. I don't feel like talking none. But he gets it out of me what happened. Then he whacks me on the side of my head. He says I shouldn't worry 'bout it now.

"Can't ya see ya gotta be tough to survive in this damn patchtown," Buzzy says.

I tell him okay. I spit the tobacco out of my mouth into the yard before I go in the house.

Cabbage is cooking on the coal stove. My ma is at the zinc table wrapping pieces of ground meat into cabbage leaves, which is what us pollocks call "pigs in a blanket." I'm hungry as hell, but my guts felt twisted up since we walked away from that drainage and I don't feel much like eating. My ma's bitching that the twins ain't back from 40 rock dump with the coal for tonight. She says it's getting damn late.

"They'll be alright," my sister Lottie says. "Them kids been going down there since this damn strike started six months ago."

Lottie's next oldest to Buzzy. She's almost seventeen and don't take no shit. She got long hair, dark as percolator coffee and bright green eyes. She's so pretty most everybody takes her shit—'cept for me and Buzzy. We laugh and tell her she must think she's the Queen of England always running round pulling back her hair and pushing her tits together in the kitchen mirror.

My ma's stirring cabbage leaves into tomorrow's soup and yelling for me and Buzzy to go down the rock dump and get the twins.

"Stop foolin with your tresses, she tells Lottie. "Get them potatoes ready. We're gonna set down to eat soon as them twins get back."

Buzzy's idling in the parlor. I go in and sit down next to him. He's already got dry pants on and his bare feet propped up on the sofa. The baseball's on the radio, but he don't look to be listening none.

"I ain't goin to no slag heap to git them twins," he yells to our ma. "Send Johnny!"

Now, I know this is crazy, cause Johnny's eight but he's slow in the head. He probably couldn't find the rock dump, let alone the twins, and sure not his way home even if he did get there.

I poke Buzzy in the ribs and ask him what he's thinking. Ask him if he's drunk. He shushes me with his finger and pulls me closer to him on the sofa.

"Quiet!" he says to me. "I don't wanna us seen outside the house no more tonight."

My mother yells again from the kitchen about fetching Esther and Frankie. Buzzy jabs his fingertip into my chest, keeping me on the couch.

"Send Johnny down there," he yells to our ma, "he don't do shit all day."

My ma drops the lid back on the soup pot. She comes stomping into the parlor. She's a big woman and heavy, so the floor squeaks when she walks. When she comes in the parlor she's glaring and the floor sounds like somebody's killing a rat.

She's yelling at Buzzy for being so selfish and so lazy. Then she sees that my face is all cut and swolled.

"Chester Pistakowski," she says to me. "What the hell happened to you?"

I look at Buzzy, then at the radio and finally at the big crucifix up on the parlor wall. I start to say something about scrapping with some boys from 37, but my ma don't let me talk. She just starts in on Buzzy, telling him that he's no good, telling him he'll get me in deep someday.

"Wuzza fair fight," is all Buzzy says to our ma.

I can see him rubbing his fingers together like he got nerves. He's looking out the window, watching the street. He ain't even looking at our ma no matter what kind of stuff she says to him.

In the middle of getting yelled at, Buzzy just gets up and drifts into the kitchen. My ma follows him, but she should know not to keep on Buzzy like that when he's getting pissed, cause he'll take a poke first and he ain't going to confession no time soon.

Staring outta the kitchen window, Buzzy finally says something. He says, "Them twins is back."

I race over to the window and look out and I see Esther and Frankie coming down through the yard past the shithouse and the chicken coop. They're near ten, but stooped over carrying them flour sacks of coal from the rock dump.

When they come in, my ma gives 'em hell for taking so damn long.

"How younz gonna stay in fourth grade if ya can't even fetch coal?" she says.

Frankie shrugs and takes the coal down to the bin in the cellar. Esther stands in the middle of the kitchen fisting up the linen of her dress. She's shouting about how they had to go behind Third Street cause the Pinkertons is all up and down Second.

"Whatcha mean the Pinkertons?" Buzzy asks. He looks at Esther with his lips curled and his eyes pinned. I can see he's wound up but good.

Frankie comes running back up from the basement, all excited. He says, "They was on horses coming up Second Street. We watched 'em from behind Zachek's chicken coop. They was banging on doors. Going into houses. They was gettin men out in their yards."

"Give some a beatin," my sister Esther says, her eyes wide.

"How bad a beatin?" I ask.

Buzzy grabs hold of my shirt.

He says, "Don't worry how bad a beatin."

He pulls me across the kitchen to the stairs and sets me on my ass on the bottom step. Yanking onto my ear, he pulls my face right in breathing distance of his, so no one can hear what he's gonna tell me. He pushes his finger hard into my cheek right below the cut.

"You're going into the attic," he says. "You I gotta wait till I come for you, Chester."

Buzzy scowls and he pushes his mouth up to my ear and says real soft, "This ain't no bullshit. Ya know these is hard men. You do what I tell ya."

"Okay," I says.

Buzzy steps back and he stands up. He says to everyone, "Chet's already been in one fight today. He don't need to be in another one."

My ma is blessing herself. I can see that she don't believe a word of this, but she ain't gonna ask no questions neither.

"Don't be sayin nothin 'bout Chester," she points her finger at the twins.

I don't like to be chickening out of nothing, but I ain't gonna argue with Buzzy neither. I scram up the steps and open the door to the attic. I'm trying to get the steamer trunk pushed over so I can reach the ladder to get into the attic when Lottie comes trotting up the stairs. Turning to face her, I take a deep breath thinking she's come to give me hell for causing trouble. But she puts a roll in each of my hands. She says, "I thought you might be hungry."

I take a bite of one of them rolls and tell her thanks. She flashes her green eyes down at the linoleum on the floor of the hall. Pushing her foot around she says, "Chester, ya gotta be careful running with Buzzy. He ain't bad exactly, but he's so fulla mad that he don't always think 'bout what's gonna happen."

I think I understand what she means, but I can't say nothing against Buzzy. I just tell her thanks for the rolls again. She gives me a smile and helps me push the trunk over to the ladder. When she goes back down the stairs to help my ma, I hear 'em the dishes clatter as they get the supper on the table.

I climb up the ladder and push the whitewashed board away from the opening and yank myself up into the attic. It's dark and cool enough I wanna go back down to the kitchen and ask Buzzy for his coat. Instead, I light up a candle and put the board back. There's a couple of boxes of shit my ma brought up from West Virginia lying round and I drop my ass onto one of them.

I'm setting there quiet chewing up the rest of them rolls, which is hard work cause my jaw hurts like hell when I open my mouth. I'm hoping my jaw ain't broke. I wouldn't mind so much a scar from this cut, cause that'd look pretty hard and all. But a broken jaw. No thanks.

After them rolls is gone, I'm still hungry and I'm getting bored of setting. I can smell the dinner cooking down there, the cabbage and meat. I'm listening real careful to what's going on downstairs, but all I hear is the sounds of them eating supper. They don't talk much but I'm right above the kitchen, so I can hear them banging round plates and bowls.

I'm thinking 'bout the first time I seen the Pinkertons. It was back April of this year, 1922, right after this coal strike started up and Buzzy and me was walking home from the first big union meeting out on Gerula's farm. Them Pinkertons come into town on horses, and we watched them ride down Joe Smolko and Lefty Jankowsky who was both motormen out Eureka 37. They chased them right up Ninth Street past Eureka Store. When they caught them, them Pinkertons busted Joe and Lefty up with a blackjack good. Beat them till their faces was so swolled they couldn't see nothing. Buzzy told me that was revenge for the two of them wrecking a motor on the way into number 37 mine the first day of the strike so nobody could go down there to work.

"Open up, ya damn pollocks!"

I hear somebody saying this and I crawl over to the side of the attic where there's a little slatted window at the peak of the roof. Looking out from 'tween the slats I can see these Pinkerton bastards on my neighbor's porch. There's two of them in their blue suits all dolled up to look like police. They're beating the door with a blackjack and yelling for Ol Man Kosturko to come out. I wanna say maybe they ain't opening up cause them's Hungarians in that house not pollocks, but I see two more of these sunsabitches ride up to our house on dark horses.

These two climb down and make for our front door. The one is tall and heavyset with a mustache that comes down past his mouth. He's already got his blackjack out and he's slapping it against his leg. The other sunafabitch is sawed-off and none too steady on his feet. The big one starts cracking his blackjack into our door.

"C'mon, ya pollocks," he says. "Open up this goddamn door."

I hear feet shuffling across the floor and the key turning in the lock. I shift myself forward so I can get a better look at what's going on. I watch the door open a crack and see a wedge of light shining onto the porch.

Then the fat sunafabitch drops his shoulder into our door and it goes flying back, the doorknob smashing up against the wall. My ma's shouting high pitched and these bastards rampage their way into our house. I hear furniture getting splintered and dishes shattering. There's screaming and these no good bastards is calling my ma a stupid Pollock bitch.

"Where's your husband?" one's asking her.

I can hear everything pretty clear cause the walls of these patchtown houses is thin as paper.

My ma's acting like she don't understand no English. She just keeps saying "*Jezus Salwowac Nam*" which is Polish for "Jesus Save Us." Listening to them cursing my ma, my stomach tightens up and my nostrils are pulling apart. I want to spring straight down and give them sunsabitches what for, but I told Buzzy I'd stick up here.

I hear a crash like a big piece of furniture getting busted up. That's when I finally hear Buzzy, his voice is loud and clear and mean as hell. It's the one he uses when somebody just got whipped bad enough for it to last a while and he ain't even near done whipping. He says, "Anythin else ya bastards want?"

There's more crashing and more yelling. Buzzy's yelling and the sunsabitches is yelling. Plates is shattering and the parlor wall shakes like the San Francisco earthquake is rattling our kitchen to pieces. Then there's a crack and everything goes pretty quiet until one of the Pinkertons says to take Buzzy outside into the backyard. I crawl over the boxes, rushing to the slat window at the other side of the attic in time to see them dragging Buzzy out the back door.

Both of them Cossacks is covered with food and their uniforms is tore. The short one's got his lip split and the blood's run down his neck and dripped onto the front of his white shirt. Buzzy's kicking and struggling, but the big bastard's got him in some kind of rasslin hold.

"Help this boy out, Jim," the big one says.

The short one pulls out his blackjack and gives Buzzy two real quick across his belly. Buzzy coughs, but I can see he's still ready to go. The big Pinkerton must see it too, cause he jerks Buzzy's head back by the hair.

"Help him out some more, Jim."

This time the little Pinkerton gives Buzzy the blackjack across his knee. Buzzy's got his face all screwed up and he's hollering like it hurt pretty good.

"One more time."

After another crack at Buzzy's knee, the big bastard Cossack lets him go and shoves him forward into the yard. He stomps on Buzzy's hand and asks him what he knows about miners chasing scabs home from Eureka 40.

Buzzy just groans and tells him to go piss up a tree. The little one says he probably don't know nothing anyhow. He says that pollocks is just too stupid to cause that much trouble. Then each of them bastards gives Buzzy a kick in his belly before they go peacocking back through the yard to their horses. Buzzy's still laying there, his bare feet wiggling outta the legs of his dungarees, when them bastards climb up into the saddle and clomp away down Second Street towards the pick-me store.

Three

Buzzy's limping pretty good, but he's better off than some of the other fellas heading up the boneyard ridge to the union meeting. A couple of men got their arms broke and one fella can barely walk. A couple more got shoulders that's all banged to hell. Most everybody living down 40 Patchtown is flush with bruises or cuts or their faces are all swolled. Ol Man Kosturko, he's got a big white bandage covering up his whole head.

We're taking the back way up to Gerula's orchard. We heard they got organizers and big union men coming down from district headquarters this afternoon to help us figure out what to do about these damn Cossacks putting their boots to us. That's if our fellas can even get past all the new thugs the damn Berwinds has brung in.

For a week now, fresh Pinkertons been coming in by the dozen. We seen them loafing around the train station down Windber. We seen their spotters, too. We watched them standing out there in front of the Palace Hotel with their hands in their pockets and their eyes keen on the streetcar, peeled strict for anybody headed into town on the union's nickel.

It's no secret them Berwinds had their feet to us miners' throats ever since this strike started up. Between the Black List and the Pinkertons and tossing folks out of the company's houses and them owning every damn thing in town from the Burgess to the rock dump, they kept us in our place, and good. But since they found that dago's body in McKluskey's drainage behind the 40 mine last week, things has gone straight to hell. Cossacks is crowding round thicker than horse flies on shit. We heard they're even bringing them in from far as Pittsburgh.

I 'spect them sunsabitches must have got wind of this meeting somehow, cause they're watching everything extra close today. Baldy says he heard they even got a road block set up out on 160 headed into town. E.J. and the rest of them Berwinds don't want none of our fellas coming into Windber—which everybody knows is just "Berwind" with the letters mixed up.

Cause Baldy and Stash live down 37, they ain't been catching no beatings. So they're all lighthearted, fooling around. They been tossing a ball back and forth over Ol Man Kosturko's broken head the whole way from Meckley's Field to New Ashtola. I walk beside Buzzy who's got a stick up under his arm like a crutch. He's blanketing the white tops of that Queen Anne's lace with tobacco juice and saying he's going to murder the deputies that give him the beat down.

Once we get to spitting distance of Gerula's, one of the oldtimers yells at Baldy and Stash to stop fooling around. They give him the raspberry, but when they start tramping down the footpath to the orchard where Gerula's letting us have the meeting, they're settled.

Down in the middle of them apple trees, I can see men from 41 and 42 Patchtowns and some Slovaks from 30 and 35. There's Eye-tailyan miners from 32 and a couple of fellas from out 38. Some of them miners got swolled lips or black eyes but none of them look to be catching it like we are down 40.

"Ya boys are lookin rough," says one of the Slovaks from 38 Patchtown.

"They been hittin us pretty good," Ol Man Kosturko tells him.

I recognize some of the trapper boys what used to live down 40 'fore the Pinkertons give 'em their papers back in August. I worked with them pulling air traps deep in 40 mine before Buzzy got me on with him loading mule cars on the B seam last fall. Looking thin, them trapper boys is over with their pas hunting in the leaves, scrounging for apples that's left over from the harvest last month. Them boys live in the Tent City back behind McKluskey's now. They're camped out down there in chicken coops and tents that's left over from the war. I give 'em a nod and they gimme a nod back.

"Boys makin it alright?" Baldy asks them.

"No use kickin," one says.

"Depends who yer kickin," Buzzy tells him, hobbling away.

The bunch of us follow Buzzy over to the other side of the orchard where one of the union men is talking Polish. Men are worried and everybody's asking what we can do 'bout all these fresh Cossacks come into town.

The organizer says that bringing the union in is the only way we'll get any rights at all from these Berwinds. He says they're gonna keep cheating us long as they can.

"I know they're bringin the Cossacks in on ya!" he says. "That's the only way they'll keep this union out!"

Then he starts yelling out all the stuff we're trying to get outta the Berwinds by striking.

"Ya men want to get honest weight for yer coal?" he asks. And miners says back, "Damn right, we want honest weight!" and then he says, "Ya want pay for the deadwork?" and men says, "Damn right, we want pay!" This goes on till he gets through all the stuff we're striking for. A contract to be in the union, no more secret pay lowering, checkoff for the union dues. Every time he says something new, men shout back that's what they want.

I seen this lots of times before, but a good many of the miners from 40 ain't doing no shouting back. Some are just standing over at the edge of the crowd looking scared. Others is grouped together in two's and three's whispering about slitting the Cossacks' throats and going after the Berwinds with dynamite.

When that organizer's done, another fella gets up and starts making the same speech all over again in Hungarian. Buzzy says that we're wasting our time here. I don't understand no Hungarian anyway, so I head over to look for apples with them trapper boys from the Tent City.

While we're grubbing in the leaves, a car comes rumbling up Ashtola Road. Some of the miners try melting into the line of oak trees at the edge of the orchard. I figure they remember the meeting back in May where the Berwinds had the Staters roll in and haul everybody off to Somerset to the jailhouse. But when the miners see a couple union men go over to meet the car, everybody comes running right back.

Mikey and me race over to the car to see who's getting out. We recognize one of the men right off, cause he's John Brophy, head of the union up in Cresson. He come down here a couple of times before. He got slicked-back silver hair and a black necktie over a clean shirt. He's smiling at everybody and waving. The other fella is younger, maybe twenty-five. He's got bright blond hair that's blowing in the wind, a square face and big shoulders. He's wearing a necktie too, but it's just hanging round his neck loose. He's watching Mr. Brophy and flashing us his bright teeth.

All the miners gather round the car, pushing, trying to get in closer. Buzzy slides up behind me and says they just wanna get in tight next to Brophy in case he come down to hand out the strike relief in person. Baldy and Stash laugh, but some of the men look at Buzzy hard, like he's a kid who's talking too damn much. Buzzy might have a point 'bout the strike relief though, cause I'm looking at everybody's clothes and they're looking like they ain't held together with nothing but coal dust.

"How ya men doin?" Mr. Brophy asks.

He slams the car door and walks over into the middle of the orchard. The younger fella gets a wood box outta the back of the car and carries it behind him. Men come up to him while he's walking, and everybody says that we're hanging tough and we ain't licked yet and stuff like that.

When they get to a spot of ground where the orchard is still all seedlings, the younger fella sets the wood apple box down and Mr. Brophy climbs up on top of it. The men step back and give him a little room. He looks out over the crowd of miners who's mostly quiet now.

Mr. Brophy says, "I come down here from Cresson cause I heard them Berwinds has brought in fresh Cossacks to give ya the beat down."

His voice is high, but loud and all the miners listen when he talks, which is kinda funny cause a lot of these miners can't understand no English.

"Well, boys," Mr. Brophy says. "I'm here to tell ya, ya brung it on yourselves!"

The men start looking at each other kind of confused. There's lots of whispering and mumbling. Men from all the different patchtowns are saying like, "What ya mean, John?" and such.

"Yer playin the Berwind's game!" he says to us. "Goin after their shittin scabs with violence."

I'm near holding my breath, while Mr. Brophy talks.

"Berwind's whole goal is to paint us union men up like crazy foreigners. Get folks thinking our union ain't nothing but a bunch of no good criminals who'll murder a man without thinking twice," he says. "The Berwinds are winding us up like a watch."

He says how violence just gives the governor good reason to send another mob of State Policers into Windber and get rid of the union once and for all. He says this is how they done for steel mill fellas three years back in Pittsburgh, how they done for them boys in Homestead. Mr. Brophy says they'll do anything to keep on paying us slave wages.

"Ya men wanna know what them Berwinds done to get them scabs to come here in the first place?" he asks us.

I look back behind me through the crowd and even though not too many men say that they want to know, Mr. Brophy pulls a folded-up piece of newspaper outta the pocket of his suit coat. He yells into the crowd of miners calling for somebody that can read the Eye-tailyan.

One of the dago miners from 32 tramps up to where Mr. Brophy is standing on his box. I watch Mr. Brophy unfold the paper and give it to the Eye-tie.

"Tell these men what that advertisement says," Mr. Brophy says.

The Eye-tie from 32 is all beaming, excited to show off for his buddies he can read. Smiling over the crowd, he says, "Dis paper say 'Brand new mine. Just opened. Five hunnerd miners needed. No less den 12 dollars a day for every man. No labor troubles.'"

"Where's it say that nice new mine is?" Mr. Brophy asks him.

"Windber, Pennsylvania."

The dago ain't smiling no more and the men who can understand English start hollering right off. Then the Eye-ties start hollering cause the fella from 32 repeats what he said to them in dago. Before long the Polish and the Slovaks and Hungarians too all understand how Berwind is tricking them scabs into coming out here.

Men are shoving their fists in the air saying we oughtta march to Windber right now. They're shouting we oughtta go down to Ninth Street and dynamite the Berwind's Big Office right away.

"Eureka Stores too! Blow all them Berwinds sky high!" says one hunkie from 42.

Mr. Brophy only lets this go on for a couple of minutes before he gets back up on his wood box. He holds his hands up in the air to quiet everybody down and his young fella goes over to the car and lets the horn blast till they do.

"I know how ya men feel about these bastards," Mr. Brophy says. "Ya wanna get 'em with the dynamite. Get 'em with the black powder!"

All the men shout, "Hell ya! Let's gittem! Let's gittem now!"

Mr. Brophy says, "I wanna get 'em too. I wanna get 'em good."

All four hundred men in the orchard start up shouting and hollering about how to get shots in on the Berwinds till Mr. Brophy puts his hands up for them to quiet down and starts back talking hisself.

"That's why we gotta be smart," he says. "Why we can't take the bait."

He tells us that the Berwinds will do anything to keep the Windber mines non-union. He says they're dirty sunsabitches with all kinda tricks up their shitty sleeves. He says that sometimes they're succeeding.

"Take the other night," he says. "Younz all know a scab got killed out behind Eureka 40. Beat in the head out on one a them farms."

I look up at Buzzy and then slip my head around for a peek at Stash and Baldy. I feel my heart thudding in my chest and my gut starting to turn. My hands are sweating till my palms are so damp they're almost wet like.

"It's just that kinda foolishness makes it easy for the Berwinds to show us out no damn good."

Mr. Brophy says that the fella what got killed didn't speak no English. Two weeks off the boat and he answered that ad in some dago newspaper in Perth Amboy. Dumb bastard didn't even know he was scabbing. I can feel my mouth dropping open and my throat getting tight. A line of bile cuts across my stomach and sweat start running down my back. All at once I want to step forward and explain it to Mr. Brophy how the whole business what happened with the scab was an accident, how nobody meant to kill him, that we was in the dark our own damn selves.

Buzzy reaches out and grabs me by my hand like to hold it. But instead he squeezes it, hard, hard. So hard that it hurts enough I might cry. He bends down and brings his mouth to my ear and I can feel his razor stubble brushing against my earlobe.

"Don't you say a word, Chester," he says to me. "Not a god damn word."

I give him a little nod and Buzzy eases up on my hand some. I look back up at Mr. Brophy perched on his apple box.

"Now, I know it ain't no union men that done this," he says stern, but almost like he knows he's lying. "But ya can bet the company's gonna say it was, to make the union men out as murderers."

Buzzy ain't let go of my hand and he's shaking his head. I see his lips crease up like he's clenching his teeth fit to bite through a pick handle. I make a face, but he doesn't say nothing, just spits into the dried-out leaves and looks back up toward Mr. Brophy, who's pointing his thumb at the blonde fella with him. Mr. Brophy says his name is Charlie Dugan and he's a union organizer from New Jersey. He's the one what found out about that advertisement for them scabs.

"He's gonna be stayin down here helpin younz out with the strike."

Mr. Brophy steps down and shoves Charlie Dugan towards the apple crate. I try a couple of times to jerk my hand loose of Buzzy's and when he finally lets go of me, I take a couple of steps off to the side. Balanced on the downslope next to one of the hunkies from 38, I watch Charlie Dugan climb up onto the crate. He looks a little nervous up there for a second, but after he gives a little cough, he settles right in and ya can tell that he must be pretty used to talking to folks gathered round like this. He says that the Berwinds got another train of scabs coming into 40 Patchtown tomorrow night.

"Ya know what we're gonna do 'bout that train," he shouts. "We're gonna get out there on the hard picket line! Ain't one of them men getting off that train won't know these Berwind mines are struck mines. Ain't a one won't know these mines are gonna be union mines!"

A lot of the miners start to yell 'bout how they'll picket for all they're worth, that they'll let them scabs know what's what, but I notice that some fellas ain't been paying no attention to what Mr. Brophy or Charlie Dugan been saying. They're still whispering about making a midnight run to the powdershed to loose up the black powder and the dynamite and have a Big Office Demolition Party.

Craning my neck round to see who's saying what, I see Baldy and Stash talking close with each other, almost whispering. Buzzy heads over towards them yanking out his tobacco plug from the pocket of his britches. He offers them each a bite from the plug in turn and when they're all set we turn back down Ashtola Road. I walk with them, but I keep off to the side with hands pushed down into the pockets of my own britches and don't ask Buzzy even for a chaw.

Four

The beatings we're catching down 40 must have got miners in every Patchtown pretty damn riled, cause there's maybe a thousand men waiting at the station for the scab train from South Fork. Miners are everywhere. Crowded between the soot stained buildings. Jammed in close to the high tipple. Pushed up against the doors of the motor barn. Some are carrying signs and working on the chants, but there's more than a passel of fellas just sniffing the sulfur smoke, looking mad as hell and ready to go. They're snarling there ain't no chance these scabs don't know they're scabbing on us.

I'm waiting for Buzzy with Baldy and Stash on the high ground to the side of the big yellow brick powerhouse where they make the electricity for 40 mine. Balanced on the heaped up slag, we're watching the girls what come down to the station with their mothers. The girls wear gingham and old flour sack dresses and the ladies got theirselves tucked into house coats and thready print dresses. They're all clutching onto the pennies and bread crusts they brung down here to hold out and offer the scabs. Like to shame them, saying you're so poor ya have to steal our men's jobs, maybe we can give ya something.

Over by the sand shed, Charlie Dugan is tryin to buck up the fellas from 40 what been getting walloped by the Pinkertons. Some of them look awful banged up, but he's shouting and yelling and it ain't long before he's got a whole crew pushed in close to the tracks chanting "Struck Mines!" and hoisting up block letter signs saying PAY FARE WAGES! and MINE ON STRIKE! Course I know some of them fellas been into the corn liquor since lunchtime and more than a few come down here hoping to kick them scabs' asses straight up between their shoulders if they set one blessed foot off that train.

Down at the 40 Little Office where we get our scrip, there's maybe ten Pinkertons scrambling round outside like headless chickens. They don't look none too happy to see the whole lot of us miners all keyed up. One of the big bastards from the Coal and Iron Police comes running outside the office yelling at a couple of them Little Office Pinkertons and jerking his thumb over at a cluster of miners around the motor barn. Then he yanks hisself up onto a big black Cossack horse. Jabbing his spurs into the bay's flanks, he wheels that horse around and tears hell for leather back towards Windber.

Curious, I watch the Pinkertons he yelled at check their guns and cinch up their belts before they start stalking up the tracks toward the motor barn. All the rest of them guards just fall back inside the Little Office.

Still waiting for Buzzy before we go down to the picket line, I ask Baldy what he thinks about the scab that got killed in the drainage ditch. Him and Stash grab hold of my arms and yank me back behind the pump house.

"Chet," Baldy says to me. "Ya can't be talkin 'bout that."

"Nobody heard me," I tell him. "'Sides I just asked what ya thought about it."

"I tell younz what *I* think about it," Stash turns his head around to make sure there ain't nobody standing close enough to hear us. "I think we're damn lucky ain't none of us setting down the Somerset jailhouse."

Baldy nods. "That ain't no shit, Chester."

He crosses his arms and looks over at Stash. Stash and Baldy are both older than me and I like running with them, but I sure don't care for both of them are staring at me like I'm some kinda dope like Mikey and they have to tell me what to do.

Stash says to me, "Anybody asks where ya was that night, ya tell 'em ya went up Ashtola to swipe apples outta Ol Man Gerula's barn."

I look down and tell Stash okay and he gives me a quick pat on the shoulder. I ain't gonna say nothing to them now for sure, but I keep dreaming about that scab splashing round in the ditch behind 40. I'm on the muddy bank, heaving bony pieces through the air at his thin arms and narrow chest, but when the chuncks hit, they just melt and run down his pit vest like black wax till the whole ditch is plumb full and it's running over the bank up onto my boots. When I wake up I can smell that drainage in my nose, stinking so bad it's like I been sleeping in McKluskey's ditch, like it's *me* crashed down and stretched out flat, dead in that dark water.

When Buzzy comes wobbling down Third Street, we all step out from behind the pump house. He's still limping some, but he's whistling and smiling like he gotta hijinks up his sleeve.

He struts over to us and gives Baldy a poke in the ribs. Baldy punches him back a quick one, but Buzzy just laughs. He lifts up his shirt and shows us he's gotta big Y slingshot stuck in the waist of his pants.

"Now whatcha gonna do with that, Buzzy?" Baldy asks him.

"Ya just wait and see what I do with this, Baldy Chenesky."

We follow Buzzy into the knot of miners in between the powerhouse and the 40 station platform. The train's already due and everybody's getting anxious. We start up yelling with the other miners.

"We're union MEN and the union's SWELL. EJ Berwind can burn in HELL."

In the middle of my own yelling, I turn round to get a look at all the men shouting and carrying on behind me. It's good to see so many miners come out to picket this train and let them scabs know these mines are struck, let them know they shouldn't even think of getting off that train in 40 Patchtown. We're fuming from the passenger tracks the whole way back to Patchtown Road.

Over to the left, past the tipple, I see that the some of the Pinkertons what come from the Little Office have snuck up all the way up past the motor barn to the yellow line of mantrip cars in front of the shifter's shanty. I watch the biggest Pinkerton scuffle his flabby body up onto the deck of one of them mantrip cars.

He starts clanging his billy on the handrail screaming for all of us miners to get the hell outta here.

"This train depot is company property," he yells to us. "Every damn one of you is guilty of trespassing."

All the men shout him down, telling him to go to the devil. We know that the train station belongs to the town and we can stand here if we like.

"Don't be trying none of your greenhorn tricks on us!" we tell him.

Mr. Dugan even walks right up to the edge of the mantrip car almost nose-to-nose with that Pinkerton and says we got as much right to be here as the Pinkerton does. When some miners from 40 come up behind Mr. Dugan and curse the Pinkerton out fierce telling him that we got *more* rights, cause he don't even live here, the other Pinkertons start getting nerves and they climb up onto the car to get away. I'm glad to see the Pinkertons put back on their heels for a change, but them miners talking that way is sure getting that fat Pinkerton fierce vexed. He shuffles right to the edge of the flat car.

He says, "All of ya pollocks will get yer due when McMullen comes down from Windber."

Now, McMullen is the new head Cossack they brung in from the Homestead strike to straighten us out after the scabs started getting chased home from the mines. Everybody knows he's the bastard behind all the beat downs, but when the miners hear 'bout him coming to fix us now, they're all laughing cause there's so few Pinkertons and so many of us miners. Somebody yells that McMullen can "go shit in his hat," and all the men hearty it up pretty good. They say it might improve the look of his head. But the chief Pinkerton gives them the evil eye and tells them they'll be settled with later.

"Come down here and settle up with me now ya got such big balls," says a skinny bearded fella from 35. I don't know him too good, but I recognize him from Buzzy telling me to watch out for him, cause he'll slip four bits to the shift boss for a better place on the seam.

The other guards up on the car are looking at one another and backing away from the edge. When more miners gather round and push in close, they pull their billies and clutch them at their legs. There's maybe twenty-five miners circled in around the mantrip car egging them guards to come on down. Mr. Dugan tries to get everybody calmed down, but not too many miners is even pretending to listen to him. I know some of them fellas got hammers stashed up under their jackets, and they're awful hot for them guards to come down into the crowd to give them what for.

"Chet," Buzzy yanks at my sleeve. "Let's join the party."

I follow Buzzy's eyes down to where he's gripping the sling shot. Outta his britches pocket, he pulls a handful of cast iron rail nuts.

"I told ya fellas I'm gonna settle up with them Cossacks," he says.

Baldy and Stash laugh, but before Buzzy can load one of them nuts up in the sling, the train whistle sounds, and everybody rushes back over to the platform to wait for the scab train. Over my shoulder, I watch them Pinkerton guards slip down off the mantrip car. They hotfoot it back to the Little Office ducking theirselfs behind the line of two tonners.

Miners crowd in thick and tight all up and down where the track pushes close to the platform and there's even more back behind. Patches of miners is grouped the whole way from the sandhouse on the other side of the high tipple to the spot the passenger tracks deadend in front of the pick-me store.

When we see the first flash of lights from the scab train shine out around the Paint Creek bend, all our signs go back up in the air and we're all shouting and hollering for all we're worth. Stash and Baldy rush down a little slope to get in with the miners who's pushing closest into the platform as the train's rolling in. The screech of the locomotive brakes drowns out all the shit everybody's saying and some of the women cover up their ears. We watch the sparks fly up off the tracks. Miners spring back behind the platform line.

I wait with Buzzy over at the corner of the powerhouse. He says he ain't going down into the crowd on account of his knee being screwed up. He takes a mouthful of corn whiskey and we watch the train squeal to stopped. Most of the miners and a lot of their wives too push down flush against the train and start shouting for the scabs to go the hell home.

Buzzy and me watch the old women and even some of the girls spit on the train and the men pound it with their fists. When the scab herders open up the doors to get a look at the crowd, some of the fellas toss rocks and bottles and they clatter off the metal loud as you please.

Buzzy says, "Damn scab herders is too yella to come out."

It looks like Buzzy might be right cause they shut the train doors up tight quick. Everybody cheers when the train gets hit by some more rocks and even a couple of bricks from some hard fellas Stash knows from down 37.

"Buzzy," I says watching this. "Ya think there's any chance it's like ol Brophy says?" I can't say Mr. Brophy in front of Buzzy, not if I want to keep all my teeth. "They're just trying to get us to take the bait."

"Chet," Buzzy says, "use yer head."

Buzzy smacks me in the chest with the pint bottle he's drinking from. "That kind a shit's all well and good for Brophy and Dugan and the rest a them Johnny Bulls. No matter how this strike comes out, we're still pollocks and hunkies and dagos and they're still ridin round in cars wearin neckties."

Buzzy backs up behind the corner of the powerhouse, out of sight of the train platform, and slaps the liquor pint into my hand. He says, "If we're gonna get shit outta these bastards, we gotta fight like hell."

I nod to Buzzy and spin the cap off the bottle. I take a quick taste of the corn liquor which is strong and burns down my throat. I look up the high blackened wall of the powerhouse which is long as McKluskey's barn and more than twice as tall.

"What about the dago we kilt?" I ask Buzzy.

"Piss on him!" Buzzy says. "The only way we're gonna win this strike is to keep it so hot them Berwinds can't get nobody to come to Windber. Make it as hot for them as they're makin it for us."

I give Buzzy a nod, but I ain't so sure I know what to think.

I round the corner and take a peek down at the platform. It's getting on dark and the electric lights on the tipple and conveyors shine down onto the crowd and the scab train, giving the whole mess a yellow glow. Cursing and grumbling and heaving chunks of bony up at the car, that corn liquor maybe catching up to them, miners are getting even rowdier than they was when the train fresh come in. It seems to me we're making it hot for them scabs, but not for the Berwinds. I spot Charlie Dugan down by the last train car in front of the sand house. Some of the *studda babas* around him is singing hymns and he's trying to follow along with them old women, but you can see he's distracted by all the fellas cursing and throwing stuff and he don't know enough Polish anyway, so he ain't doing so good.

Both the singing and the yelling eases up when folks spy the headlights from McMullen's long black deputy car rolling up the road from Paint. We watch that sedan round the big curve at the top of 40 Hill and rumble down its way the whole way down Patchtown Road. As the car drifts in towards the Little Office, folks quiet down flat and watch it putter to a stop.

When McMullen flings open the door and gets out of the sedan, he's decked out in some kinda fancy outfit and it's like all of us together draw a deep breath. Short haired and wiry, that Pinkerton's sporting a big bristly mustache and two rows of brass buttons running the whole way down his blue-dye wool coat and yellow murderer's stripes stitched to the seam of his pants. Them other Pinkertons come racing out of the Little Office saluting the sunafabitch like he's General Grant, but he don't pay a shred of mind. He just shifts his slouch cap, goes round to the back of the sedan and snatches up an armload of rifles from the trunk and slaps them into the hands of the Cossacks. He barks at them deputies, cajoling all of them to get their donkey asses into that car. When the sedan's plumb stuffed, he jumps back behind the wheel and spins up a mess of coal dust, jerking back away from the Little Office and onto Patchtown Road toward the train platform.

Without so much as a horn blast, McMullen wrenches the deputy sedan off the road into the railyard till he's running slow and steady up against the crush of miners swelled back away from the train. Folks are yelling and cussing and tripping over their feet to get out of the way, but McMullen just keeps right on going, pushing the whole crowd with the big chrome grill till that sedan's bumper is right up flush to the train. When the scab herders roll open one of the railcar doors, the two Pinkertons inside point their shotguns out over the crowd. I'm thinking that McMullen is one cold operator, getting his whole passel of Cossacks all the way from the Little Office to the train car without saying a single word.

Like he can't wait no longer to give it to us miners, McMullen's the first one stomping outta the sedan. He's grabbing and pulling the rest of them deputies out of the sedan, cursing and cuffing them cross the shoulders to get up onto the train car. The two scab herders reach them down a hand while the other Pinkertons keep their shotguns trained on us.

Standing back on the slag heap away from the tracks with Buzzy, I can see Charlie Dugan working his way through the *studda babas* over to where the Cossacks are climbing up into the train, but them old ladies are bunched in thick and they're slow moving, so Charlie don't even get far as the tipple before every one of the deputies what rode over from the Little Office are perched up in the train car and pointing them rifles down at us.

Lodged right in the middle of all them Pinkertons, McMullen wraps one hand round the white butt of his holstered pistol and holds a sheet of grimy paper in the other. He waves that dirty paper at us, like it's the Declaration of Independence or maybe the bill of sale for the town.

"My name is Lieutenant John McMullen of the Special Police," he shouts to us miners. "I been lawfully and dutifully charged by Burgess Barefoot of Windber to clear you rabble out of the train station for preventing the passage of workers over a public thoroughfare."

Chanting "Struck Mines!" and "Scabs go home!" not a one of us miners near that platform is having this lawful and dutiful shit. A lot are just yelling that McMullen can go to hell trailing right behind old Berwind. I see a few women readying their pennies to throw at the scabs.

"There's the sunafabitch I'm after," Buzzy says.

At first I don't know what he's talking about, but once I follow Buzzy's eyes up to the rail car, I recognize the fat deputy standing left of McMullen is the same one that give Buzzy his beat down in the yard behind our house.

McMullen's snarling down at us and it's almost like there's an electric current twisting his face something fierce. I don't think even he gives no kinda shit about lawful or dutiful, cause he's spitting right down into the crowd.

"Ya sunsabitches better clear the hell outta here," he shouts. "Or you'll all pay heavier than Homestead."

Most folks are still kinda laughing, like he's gonna chase away a thousand angry miners with less than ten Pinkertons. Some of the men are talking 'bout just pulling him down off the train and give him what for.

But when the other five train car doors crash open, there's three Pinkertons in each one. Every last one of them sunsabitches are pointing shortbarrel shotguns right into the crowd. Everybody shuts up their mumbling and starts looking round at each other, like they don't know whether to sing *Anioł Pański* or go blind.

I'm mostly keeping my eye on Buzzy though, no matter what anybody else is doing. Groping some of them rail nuts outta his pants, he's already got the slingshot yanked out and ready. He peeks out from behind the corner of the powerhouse, fingering a nut into the nest and draws back the elastic. It's a pretty long shot, but Buzzy ain't no joke with a slingshot. I seen him hit rats sniffing around the sawmill the whole way from the shifter's shanty. He's got one eye closed and is sighting that portly Cossack in good.

But that's when a whole mess of motor car headlights comes glaring onto the lot of us from across Patchtown Road and we hear all their engines roar to life. Looking over, I can see there's maybe a dozen deputy cars setting there right across the street hemming us in pretty as you please. They must have come the back way past McKluskey's and snuck down First Street when everybody was over on the picket line.

"Now clear outta here ya damn stinkin pollocks," McMullen says. "We're unloading this train." He lets loose a round from his pistol and them deputy cars begin creeping towards us.

Folks start to turn away, backing theirselves down Patchtown Road. But Charlie Dugan kicks up yelling. He says, "Stay where yer at! Ya ain't done nothin wrong!" Some of them men stop, and Charlie keeps on yelling, his voice ringing out. Two big hunkies let him get up on their shoulders. "Don't let them get rid of ya that quick. Ya men tell them scabs these mines are struck mines."

While everybody's eyes is glued to Charlie Dugan, Buzzy steps back out from behind the corner of the powerhouse. He fires one of them cast iron nuts up over the crowd. It zips through the air in front of the tipple and streaks down to crack the fat Cossack right on his white forehead.

Nobody knows what happened at first, because the tubby Pinkerton just drops to his knees. But when he splashes right outta the train, all the miners laugh. That's when McMullen starts yelling for his Cossacks to give it to us.

A bunch of them Pinkertons flop down off the rail cars pronto and start whacking at the closest miners with their gun butts. It's crazy like back in the early days of the strike. Cossacks is yelling and miners is swinging at the Cossacks with hammers and sawed-off shovel handles, pick handles, anything. Cause I already been cracked in the face once this week, I'm not sure whether to get mixed up or keep clear of things. I watch Buzzy over by the tipple man's shack. He's near to braining one of them Pinkerton guards with a broom handle.

But when the Pinkertons from the line of deputy cars get into it too, it goes real bad for us, cause they're firing off the buckshot. Some of us are getting tagged and the rest is running like hell. Them shotgun blasts kick up the coal dust four and five feet in the air and a lot of them miners and their wives run towards Paint Creek, up Patchtown Road, anywhere. The ones that ain't running fast enough, they're getting clubbed with the butts of them guns.

Once all the guards from the cars has run past the powerhouse, I see my chance to get the hell away from that Cossack stew. I start running down along the tracks headed for Paint Creek, but I run smack into the back of one of them guards. I spin around and sprint for all I'm worth back up towards the station platform with that guard dashing right after me.

When I get up past the locomotive, I run in front of Charlie Dugan, and he reaches down one of his big hands and grabs hold of the collar of my pit jacket. He gives me a yank up over the latch between two of the train cars and then shoves me on through. I roll over a couple of times in the pea shale, but I don't even feel it. Getting up, I just start running again fast as I can manage down along the Paint Creek tracks and I don't look back. Not once.

FIVE

Holding court like, Buzzy's setting up at the bar of the 40 Hotel. He's got Stash and Baldy with him and they're clutching coffee mugs of beer in their hands. They been chewing over the whole business with that scab train for three damn hours. Hell, it's all they been talking 'bout for the last week and a half.

"So I give it to him, ya know," Buzzy says. "Fat bastard fell outta that train like a two-hundred-pound sack a shit. Heard they sent his ass straight *back* to Homestead."

I'm setting over by the wall with Mikey where we're playing checkers and Mikey's listening to all this close. He's saying to me how he wishes he could have been down the 40 station to see some of them guards have their turn at catching a beating. I'm thinking it weren't so bad for him that he had to go up to Vintondale to help his uncle out with his pigs.

"I dunno," I says to Mikey. "It was a pretty rough spot, and I don't know we got much from it."

It's the middle of the afternoon and there ain't too many men in the bar, so everybody setting around can hear what I'm saying. Buzzy spins round on his stool and looks at me like I lost my mind.

"Whatcha mean, Chester?" he says. "They ain't brought in one scab train since."

"Is that all ya can see, Buzzy?" I ask him. "What about all the miners that got the beat down?"

"If yer gonna eat eggs in the morning," Buzzy laughs. "Somebody's gotta break 'em open."

I don't wanna argue with Buzzy, but I can't seem to steer clear neither. I start going on 'bout how many miners and there wifes got banged up or trampled and the way the Pinkertons put the curfew on all the Patchtowns.

"How we gonna get these mines union with that goddamn McMullen hisself set up like a king right here in the 40 Little Office? He's watchin everything we do."

Everybody's looking at me now, and I can see Buzzy's gripping onto his mug real tight like he's getting ready to fling it cross the barroom at me, but some of the other men at the bar are shaking their heads like I know what I'm talking about.

"That's plenty outta you, Chester," Buzzy says.

I flash a quick look over at the men who's nodding and then my eyes go right back down to the checker board. All I want is to finish my mug of beer and get outta the damn hotel, but Mikey keeps on asking me questions 'bout the scab train beatings, who got hit, who gave it to which of them guards.

"Mikey," I says finally. "Shut the hell up!"

I raise up from the table and drink off the little bit of beer left in my coffee mug before I slap it down onto the plank wood tabletop. Everybody in the 40 Hotel barroom looks at me when I walk across the room. I don't give a damn and don't even say goodbye to nobody. I just make for the door.

When I grab hold of the cast iron handle of the frame door, Mr. Facianni, who's the barber for the Eye-tiez down Dago Town in Windber, has got his hand on the other side, like to pull it open.

I let go of the door and step over to the side, cause even though he's just supposed to be the Eye-tie barber, everybody knows he's really the boss of them Black Handers and they're nothing to fool with. They run the liquor and the number payoff through the whole county and all kinds of worse stuff too.

When Facianni sees me jump outta his way so quick, he steps back away from the door and waves his hand for me to come on out. He's wrapped in a brown suit with a necktie splitting his shirt in two and a big brown hat plopped down on top of his head.

He gives me a fake little smile and says, "C'mon boy. Let's go."

My mouth gets dry and I slip out past him quick. He tromps inside the barroom, and the two big fellas what's with him, one fat and one thin, follow right behind. From out on the porch, I sneak a peek into the window. Standing next to the bar with his feet spread wide apart, Facianni tosses his hat on one of the clothtop stools. Reaching up a bit, he drops his hand heavy down on Buzzy's shoulder. Them big dagos in suits wave Stash and Baldy off, over to the checkers table with Mikey. Then Facianni hoists hisself up onto the stool to the side of Buzzy, and the bartender pours him a coffee cup full of dark wine.

Catching a lungful of that sulfur smoke out on the porch, I watch Facianni lean his dark face in close to Buzzy's. Whatever he says, Buzzy must not like it, cause he creases his mouth and clacks his beer mug down onto bar. Facianni shrugs his shoulders and lowers hisself down off the stool to the plank floor. When he waves for them, them big dagos strut over and they all start for the door. I pull my cap down tight on my head and shag down the stairs and out onto Patchtown Road headed for Windber.

Cause they only got candles, the Hungarian church is dark as a tomb inside and I'm feeling kinda funny, cause I ain't never been to no Hungarian church before. But for what I gotta say, I don't want no Polish priests to know nothing about it. I slip up the aisle between the rows of pews and get into the line of Hungarians snaking back from the confessional door. I stand there with them hunkies, watching them go in one by one to see the priest.

When it's my turn, I shuffle in and kneel down. It's all dark wood in there and there's a varnished wood screen with square holes cut in it and a thick purple curtain. I twist the curtain over to the side a little so I can see through the holes just a little to make sure somebody's over there.

"Father," I says, "I ain't no Hungarian, but I come to confess."

The priest asks me how long it's been since my last confession, and I tell him it's been a while and we leave it at that. Then he asks me about my sins. When I don't say nothing for a bit, he asks me how old I am. I wanna tell him that I'm older, but I figure lying to the priest in confession is probably a pretty bad sin, so I give him the truth.

When he hears that I'm going to turn fifteen next month, he says there ain't nothing I could have done so bad that God can't forgive me. I can almost hear the smile sneaking into his voice like I'm some kinda dumbass come into this confession all scared and nervous just to admit about saying "Jesus Christ" too damn much or staring at some Hungarian girl's fancy ass.

So, I says to him right off, "Father, ya know 'bout that scab got killed up behind 40."

He says that he knows about it. There's a second of quiet, and then all of the smile's gone outta his voice. He says, "Son, if ya know somethin 'bout what happened up there, you gotta tell me."

"Father," I says. "I was one of the ones what chased that scab into the ditch."

I set there in the close-in dark of the confessional. I can hear that Hungarian priest breathing slow and heavy on the other side of the screen, hear him rustling his surplice. I don't know whether I should keep running my mouth or just get up out of there and leave.

"Wuz ya the one that killed him?" he asks, finally.

"No," I says. "It was my brother what killed him."

I lay it out for that priest, the whole story of how we waited for them scabs to be coming home from the mine and how we chased them through the woods. I tell him 'bout getting the smack on the jaw and how it was on accident that Buzzy got the scab on the head instead of the shoulder with the bat. I tell him it was only later we found out them dagos didn't know they was scabbing.

He listens close to all of this, asking me questions 'bout how many scabs was there and where it was Buzzy hit the dago and stuff like that. Before he gives me the penance, he makes me tell him again 'bout throwing them rocks and how come we brung the bat.

Soon as I receive the absolution, I get up and slide off into one of them Hungarian pews. I flop down on my knees and start into the whole baker's dozen of Hail Marys.

After I'm done. I pull myself up and go outside of the Hungarian church. I set down on the steps for a long minute thinking about the fella that got killed, who he might have been and the way he got brung here, but I also think about the folks on our side that the Pinkertons drug out of their houses and the ones that got the beat down at the 40 station. I wonder if maybe there's some way all of this balances itself out, but the whole thing all feels like two plus two equals five. I think some about the confession too, the way the priest asked me if I was sorry for my sins. I told that hunkie I was, but if the dago had knew he was scabbing on us, I doubt I'd feel half so bad as I do. Truth told, I don't know this confessing makes me feel a damn bit better than I did before. I can't even really say why I went. Maybe just cause it's the one thing Buzzy wouldn't of done.

Six

Four days later and the rest of the guards Berwind's sent for after the 40 Station Riot must have all come in, because they got 40 Patchtown locked down tight as the paymaster's satchel. Ain't enough McMullen's shacked up down the Little Office. Now there's horse Cossacks all up and down our streets and a whole carload of Pinkertons keeping watch at the top of Patchtown Road from the top of 40 Hill. Hell, miners can't even leave 40 at all unless they get the okay from one of them guards. For sure, we ain't gonna see no more union organizers coming our way for a good long time.

Not being much able to leave the house, Buzzy and me and Lottie and our ma just been setting, playing cards round the kitchen table, what Buzzy and me nailed back together after he broke it on the little Cossack when they came to visit. Lottie's winning for the third time this afternoon. Buzzy says she's cheating, but I don't see it. The twins is off in the parlor cutting some dolls outta the newspaper left from what me and Buzzy used to line our shoes with. Johnny's setting in the dining room chewing on the wax from an old beeswax lamp. My ma pushes the rest of her matchsticks into the center of the table.

She says, "Time to get supper started up."

Cause there ain't no more cabbage or hamburg, we're eating mush and potatoes again. Buzzy's been talking about going out and stealing a chicken from outta McKluskey's henhouse, but Lottie told him not to try it. She says everybody knows we ain't got no chickens.

"People smell that chicken cookin the whole damn way to Ashtola," she says.

"Lottie's right," ma says to Buzzy. "Ya bring enough damn trouble on yerself without bein labeled a chicken thief besides."

Buzzy smacks his fist on the tabletop and stomps off into the parlor. He grabs the rest of the newspaper from the twins. He folds it up and puts it into a box next to the cellar step. Cause Esther's only nine, she starts whining 'bout her dolls, Buzzy says they can't be pissing that newspaper away like that. He says we're gonna need it to line our shoes again when it starts to snow.

I follow Buzzy out onto the porch. He's setting down on the kindling box rolling up a bit of tobacco in a little square of newspaper he kept so's to make up a cigarette.

"Times is tough, Chet," he says to me.

He shakes his shoulders and lights the little cigarette with one of the kitchen matches. I'm thinking I don't need to be told about how times is. We ain't hardly had no meat in a week and Buzzy had to sell his radio just to get us the last round of hamburger and cabbage.

"How come we're so bad off?" I ask him.

"Where ya been?" he says. "There's a strike on."

I nod and reach for the cigarette when he holds it out to me. I take a good puff and pass it back to him.

"We been on strike for six damn months," I says. "But we ain't never been so broke we had to go short of food before."

"Damn curfew," Buzzy says to me.

"40 Mine been closed long before they started up this curfew," I says.

"Chrissake Chet! Where ya think our money been comin from?"

Buzzy tosses his head and takes a pull that burns down the rest of his cigarette. He says for me to remember when that dago Facianni come to see him in the 40 Hotel.

"He's the boss a them Black Handers," I says. "I ain't fooled that he's just some barber."

Buzzy nods and says that's exactly what he is. He tells me how them wops hired him to run a load of bootleg liquor out to Seanor every week since two months after this strike started up.

"How ya think we been gettin fed so good?" he looks right at me.

I don't know what to say to all this, but it makes some sense, for sure. I always wondered how we bought a radio in the middle of a coal strike. When I ask Buzzy what happened, he spins around so roaring mad that I scoot my ass back away to keep from getting clipped.

"Ain't ya been listenin to nothin I said, Chester?" he asks me. "Them Black Handers ain't gonna risk all their liquor gettin snatched up by a bunch of greedy curfew Pinkertons. I ain't been to Seanor in weeks."

We sit there on the porch for a couple of minutes before I stand up and lean against the banister. It's getting cold. I twist the collar of my coat up so it covers my neck some. I look down the street past the frame houses at the company store. The union told us not to shop there. Not that it matters, since we ain't got no money and EJ Berwind sure ain't offering credit to any miner on strike.

I ain't sure how Buzzy's gonna feel 'bout hearing it from me, but I ain't too keen on starving neither—so I tell him what I heard down the rock dump going through the bony looking for last night's coal chunks.

"The union got a store tent set up behind 35," I says to him. "They got flour and lard and vegetables."

"Ya need money to go to the store, Chet," Buzzy says.

"Since that Charlie Dugan come in, I heard they're offerin credit to all the strikin miners. Like them stores they set up down Saint Michael back in May."

At first, I'm thinking Buzzy won't wanna go to no union store, but when he hears there's a chance of us getting some credit, he's raring. He pinches the cigarette out between his fingers and tells me to go get my hat from in the house. He tells our ma that we're going up 35 and that we'll bring something back for supper that ought to be better than that damn mush.

My ma shakes her head and tells Buzzy to keep his eye on me and to be careful of them guards. Buzzy just laughs and says that they ought to be careful of him.

"Just don't be runnin yer mouth so much," she says.

Crouched low on the front porch, we watch them Pinkerton horses go clomping up Second Street past Kosturko's. When they make the turn into Ash Alley, me and Buzzy slip off of the porch and through the line of backyards towards Zachek's. After crossing the rail bridge over Paint Creek, we claw our way up over the 40 rock dump into the woods.

Shortcutting over the bony piles, it only takes us a half hour to get to the Slovak Cemetery, where the path breaks off towards 35. We're real high up on the ridge at the edge of the boneyard and we can see the whole way down over the hill into Windber, the paved streets and plankboard sidewalks, the yellow brick Hungarian church, the red brick Polish church, and street car tracks that run the whole way along the valley from Eureka 38 to Dago Town.

Off by itself on the opposite rise, the superintendent's big brick standalone sets back from the street, and there's a whole line of Pinkerton cars out front, near as many as we can see parked on Ninth Street between the Berwind's Big Office and the two-story Eureka Company Store for the Windber miners. Perched out on the edge of the limestone rock at the corner of the trail, Buzzy says he can see two more Cossack cars setting down on Main Street out front of the Windber train station.

Cause we made pretty good time, we hoof outta the woods and down into 35 before it's too late in the afternoon. We don't see no guards right off, but Buzzy has us keep to Railroad Street on the far side of the tracks so we can cut through the miners' yards and back into the woods if any of them Cossacks catch sight of us.

"So, where they got this store set up, Chester?" Buzzy says to me.

I tell him we gotta get over to the other side of 35, to the south corner of Horkheimer's farm. So we hike along Railroad Street trying to keep a weather eye out for the Pinkertons. But it's only miners on the streets and there ain't too many of them. I tell Buzzy I'm feeling hungry enough to eat half a pig. He says he's getting a rumbling in his stomach too and that he can't wait to get to the union store.

"Maybe they got some pierogies cookin over there," I says.

Buzzy just laughs and says we better keep on walking. So we keep on through 35 past the row of miners' frame houses and the pit boss's standalone at the end. It's a good walk till the road curves back away from the high tipple of 35.

But when we get to Horkheimer's cornfield, there ain't no tent and there ain't no cars and there ain't no miners. There ain't even no men from the union or nothing in the field. Me and Buzzy cross the road and we're standing up right in the middle of where the union store oughtta be. But there ain't a damn thing 'cept high yellow grass that's all crushed down by some tire tracks.

Buzzy kicks at the ground a couple times, and I'm waiting for him to give me hell for dragging us out here, but he don't yell or nothing, just says that we should start back.

I'm feeling starved, and I grab up a weed from the side of the road and stick it in my mouth for something to chew on. Buzzy grabs one too and we start hiking back down 35 Road till we get back to the plank sidewalks where the company doubles sprout up on both sides of us again.

First miner we see, Buzzy says to him 'bout the union store being gone. He tells us that Charlie Dugan and them had the tent set up till this morning, but then the Cossacks come in and run the union outta 35 Patchtown. They told the union men they'd set fire to the tent and everybody in it if they didn't clear the hell out.

"What happened to the store?" I ask.

"They packed up the whole thing and headed up to Mine 42."

Buzzy spits out his weed stalk and says that we're going up to 42 Patchtown. Then he turns around and starts right back down 35 road where we come from. I go chasing after him leaving that miner from 35 holding his hat. I yell to Buzzy that there ain't no way we're gonna get back from 42 before it's full dark.

"Oh, we're goin out to 42, Chester," Buzzy tells me. "I didn't come this whole damn way for nothin."

"We can't walk through the woods in pitch black," I says. "We're gonna have to go home through Windber."

"I don't give a footlong shit if we have to walk home through hell, Chester. Just so we ain't goin there empty handed."

Now Buzzy knows there ain't no way we're heading through Windber at night without running into the Pinkerton guards, but he ain't in no mood to be argued with and I sure as hell ain't in no mood to be walking the whole way back to 40 Patchtown without him.

SEVEN

It's already close to dusk when we round the 42 rock dump and finally get a peek at the union tent store. Raggedy and stained, that big green army tent sets up on a patch of scrub between 42 Road and the Pennsylvania Rail tracks that mark the county line. From the curve of the road, I can see Charlie Dugan standing between his black Ford and the union tent.

Charlie's still wearing his necktie, but his shirt's stained and his suit coat's flared open. He's got his hand on his hip talking to the miners lined up to get into the tent. I crack to Buzzy that Charlie's the one what saved me from them Pinkertons back at the train riot, but Buzzy don't much seem to care and speeds up his walking. I hurry it up after him.

"Ya hear what I said, Buzzy?"

Buzzy says that he heard me, but he don't slow down one bit. When we get to the store tent, I start hiking over to give a hello to Charlie Dugan, but Buzzy grabs me by the shirtsleeve and yanks me to the back of the line with him.

"Remember, "he says. "We're in a big damn hurry. We ain't got no time to be shooting the shit."

Waiting with the other miners, I hear everybody pissing 'bout how hard times has got with this curfew come down on us, no food and Cossacks everywhere. After Charlie disappears into the tent, some men say that the union's damn near outta money and we best get what we can get outta this store.

When it's our turn to get inside, one of the union men at the tent flap asks us for our local and Buzzy says that we come from down 40. The fella nods to us and says that Buzzy gets a full share, and since I just come off of being a trapper boy last year, I only get half. He hands Buzzy a burlap sack and we step inside the tent store.

Back against the green flaps on the far side, a couple fellas try on shoes, and in the corner some fill up their flour sacks with potatoes and cabbages. Buzzy hands our sack to me and I follow him. We shuffle over to where they got some crates of sweet potatoes stacked on the ground. We pop some of them into our sack along with a half dozen onions and cabbages. At a makeshift table one of the union men dishes us up a bit of hamburger meat wrapped in butcher's paper. I ask him where all this meat come from. He says that union men up in Cresson sent a hundred pounds of cow meat down to us for the strike relief.

"That's pretty tasty," I says to him.

I feel a hand come down on my shoulder, and when I turn around Charlie Dugan is standing there next to Buzzy. Looking a bit tuckered, Charlie's saying that all of us union men gotta stick together if we want to beat them damn operators. I know he's kinda shining me on a little bit, but I still like that he's talking to me like I'm any other union man and not like I just come off of being a trapper boy.

"Heard ya had some trouble down 35 today," Buzzy says to Charlie Dugan.

Buzzy's taller than Charlie and pushes hisself so close that Charlie has to look into his chin when he talks. Charlie cuts his eyes sideways and says that ya, they got a visit from the Cossacks. But he says he ain't too worried 'bout them coming up here cause they moved the tent store to the other side of the county line and their deputies ain't got no authority to come over into Cambria County.

"If ya think that's gonna put the brakes to them Cossacks," Buzzy laughs. "Ya been spendin too much time up in Cresson pickin out fancy suits."

Buzzy lifts up the tail of Charlie's suit coat and gives it a run between his fingers. A couple of the miners on the other side of the tent is starting to look over at Buzzy and Charlie standing there.

"Son," Charlie says. "I'm glad ya could come up here to get some meat and vegetables for your family to eat."

Charlie backs away toward the door of the tent, turns his back on Buzzy and me. Seeing there ain't gonna be no trouble, the other men in the tent turn back to what they was doing. But I step forward and push myself up in front of Buzzy.

Calling to Charlie as he's walking out, I says, "Mr. Dugan, I just wanted to say thanks for the hand ya gimme down the 40 station."

Charlie Dugan smiles at me and says that he thought he seen me before. Then he asks me if Buzzy's my brother. When I says ya, he looks over at Buzzy and gives him a smile and says again about all of us miners sticking together.

Charlie holds his hand out for Buzzy to shake, but Buzzy just tightens up his eyes and keeps them stared straight over at this one miner in the corner who's got one shoe on and one shoe off. Finally, Charlie just shrugs. He says, "See ya boys later" and walks back outta the tent.

I can't say I like the feel of Charlie walking back outta the tent by hisself and me not saying nothing to him. It ain't just that he give me the toss down the train station, but something else too. I'm trying to figure out just what's bothering me, but Buzzy grabs me by the arm and says it's getting late and we better get a move on back home quick.

We snatch up a half pound of sugar each and five of flour for Buzzy and half that for me. When we get over to the tent flap, the union man at the door says we can have a pear and an apple for each brother and sister we got, so I grab up the fruit and drop it down into the sack. Then the union man checks our sack to make sure we got our fair share before he pulls back the tent flap to let us outta there.

I'm saying thanks. Thanks to everybody. Even Buzzy says thanks once. Right before he says we gotta hurry it the hell up and get outta damn 42. He pushes the sack into my hand, and we start double quick back down toward Eureka 35.

I'm up in front and Buzzy's in back and we're shaking our legs pretty good and our feet are tapping them reddog roads click, click, click. We tear one of them pears outta the sack and split it up good. I got my half down in about a second and I'm sliding my tongue cross my chin licking up the juice drooling off the corner of my mouth. The moon's coming up big and orange as safety paint and so close it's like somebody shoved a bushel basket up in the sky above the 42 tipple.

By the time we get far enough into Windber to see the guards, I'm sweating pretty good under my pit jacket. Going out to 42 didn't even sound so good when we was back in 35 and Buzzy was saying 'bout looking like fools wasting our time coming the whole way over the boneyard ridge for nothing. But now, looking at the size of them blue suit Cossacks hovering over by the Somerset Avenue Eureka Store, I'm starting to feel like my blood is ready to run straight away right out of my veins and hightail it back to 40 Patchtown.

"Just walk natural, Chester," Buzzy says to me and I realize that with running that liquor Buzzy must be pretty used to this kind of feeling. "Them boys ain't got no idea where you're coming from or where you're supposed to be. To them you're just one more slobbering pollock."

I'm trying to look natural as I can, but I'm clutching onto our sack like for dear life till we get past them guards and make the turn onto Somerset Avenue. I let out my breath and Buzzy says I done good. He grabs the sack outta my hand and starts up whistling the "Two Tonner Polka."

Headed through the West End, there's more miners and other folks out on the sidewalks and we're kind of blending into the crowd like, but once we get up past Mihalek's Drugs by the Palace Hotel, I'm coming to see that there's near as many Pinkertons on the streets of Windber as there is haunting 40 Patchtown.

Buzzy must know a good many folks, cause all kinds of people says, "Hey, Buzzy" and "How ya doing, Buzzy?" when we're walking down the street. Buzzy barely even bothers saying "hey" back and don't pay 'em no mind. It's strange to me how he got this whole other life going that I don't know nothing about.

I'm just starting to get a little bit comfortable sneaking through town when the thinner of them dagos what come into the 40 Hotel with Facianni slides up on us from behind. He slaps his hand down onto Buzzy's shoulder and says the barber needs to talk to him pronto. Buzzy nods and right quick he pushes the sack into my hand.

"I'll be back in a minute, Chester," he says. "Just stand here and don't do nothing stupid."

Buzzy goes jogging round the corner with that dago leaving me in front of the Arcadia Theatre. I'm shifting from one foot to the other and I feel dumb as hell to be standing there by myself. All these supervisors and superintendents and bosses is going into the picture show with their wives and sweethearts and they're looking at me harsh, like what's this dirty trapper boy doing standing here on a Saturday night all by hisself in front of the Arcadia Theatre. I'm sweating out my pits and I don't like them looking at me one bit and I just try keeping to the shadows.

It seems a long damn time before Buzzy comes stomping back. He's mad as I ever seen him. He's spitting on the ground and kicking at the sidewalk and I'm half sure he's gonna smack the teeth outta my mouth just for breathing.

"Your union friend done me pretty good, Chester," he says.

"Whatcha mean?" I says.

"Sunafabitch turned me in."

Buzzy pulls open his Peacoat and shows me his inside pockets is stocked full of pears.

"Ya take them from the union tent?" I ask him.

"Damn right," he says. "I wasn't walkin all that way to get six lousy pears for the trouble."

"But we ain't the only ones that need 'em."

Quick as lightning, Buzzy slaps me cross the side of my head. His hand catches me right under my eye and I can feel my head jerk off to one side and my eyes start to tear up. But I ain't gonna cry. I bite down on my lip so hard it's all I can think about.

Buzzy looks at me for a second, then he grabs hold of my pit jacket and pulls me around the corner into Swede Street alley. He's all nervous watching me and starts brushing my hair back from where he got me with the palm of his hand. He says he's sorry one time, then another and that scares the piss outta me, cause I ain't never heard Buzzy say he's sorry for nothing.

"It ain't your fault," he says finally. "We just gotta look after ourselves."

Then he grabs me by the hand, and we start back through the alley towards Main Street. Pulling me along behind him, Buzzy tells me how Facianni clued him in that cops was looking for him all over Windber.

"They was asking all the Eye-tiez in Dago Town if they seen me."

"What ya gonna do?" I ask.

Buzzy shoves his hands deep in his pockets. He says he figures there ain't nothing he can do but hoof it back to 40 and take his chances. He says he damn sure ain't gonna go running out on the lam and there's only so long ya can hide in Windber or any of these patchtowns.

"Besides, Chester," Buzzy smiles at me. "I done took far worse a hidin from our pa than I'm ever gonna get for swipin some damn pocketful a fruit.

EIGHT

I follow Buzzy the whole way down the wood board sidewalk of Main Street still trying my red letter best to walk natural. I keep my eyes straight ahead and try not to hoof it too fast or too slow. But when we pass in smelling distance of the horse Cossacks on the corner of 12th Street, fear runs through my gut like lye. Buzzy keeps saying shit to me about the baseball, talking 'bout the shellacking Jackie Scott put on them World Series batters last month.

I whisper that I can't be talking this damn baseball cause I'm scared as hell. Buzzy says he been in some spots like this before and we just gotta make like we're a couple of miners going down the road. But the further we push into the East End, the more something don't feel right. Even for the curfew there's too many Cossacks lurking on the corners and it seems like every one of them Pinkertons has got eyes just for us.

Buzzy must feel it too, cause his eyes are twitching from guard to guard and corner to corner. His hand is gripping our sack extra tight hoofing past the line of black Ford cars in front of St. John's Polish church. He creases up his forehead and don't say another thing 'bout them New York Giants or nothing else. His head swivels round from the guard pretending to loaf in front of the 6th Street Dairy store back to the horse Cossacks closing up ranks on Main Street behind us.

"Ya sure ya just took them pears?" I says to Buzzy.

"Shit," Buzzy says. "They can have 'em."

My heart's pounding and I'm scanning all the frame house yards for some way we can get clean outta sight of all these damn guards. When I spot an open place in one of the hedges over by Kinjelko's Meat Store, I grab Buzzy's coat sleeve and start pulling at him. But before we even get two steps, a black deputy sedan comes barreling down 8th Street and screeches stopped kitty-corner in front of us.

When Buzzy sees that it's McMullen hisself propped at the wheel, his face goes white as wood ash. His jaw drops and he whips his head round for a quick gander at them horse Cossacks trotting up the street behind us.

"This ain't about no damn pears," Buzzy says to me.

He drops our sack onto the middle of the sidewalk. We look across the frame house yards for some kind of exit, but I don't see no way to get shot of them damn horses.

Looking mean as the devil, McMullen's full flung outta the car and sprinting round the front bumper. Ripping his coat open, he reaches for the gun belt round his waist. He rips that big chrome steel pistol up with both hands and points it at Buzzy and me.

"Get yer hands in the air, ya murderin pollock!" he yells to Buzzy.

I'm looking over at Buzzy. My heart's thumping fit to come straight the hell outta my chest. Buzzy puts one of his hands part way up, but I can see his eyes darting from one yard to the next, till he fixes on that hole in Kinjelko's hedge.

"You too, little pollock, get 'em up!" McMullen waves his gun at me.

I'm so scared I don't even move for a second. I just look at that big damn pistol. Then I look back over to Buzzy. He ain't moving, but I can see in his eyes, he's fixing to bolt.

Things is happening so fast that I don't really start putting two and two together till I got my hands up and

McMullen says something for the second time to Buzzy 'bout being a murderer. Then I know for sure this ain't got nothing to do with no pears, stole or otherwise. This ain't even about Buzzy slingshotting that guard down the train station. McMullen's done got wind of who killed that Eye-tie scab up behind 40 and it's time to pay the piper.

I got my hands high in the air now, but McMullen ain't even looking at me. He got his pistol pointed right at Buzzy, but Buzzy still ain't putting his other hand up. He's just holding it down by his pants and his eyes is flailing from place to place, hopping from Polish Church to the meat store hedge to the line of black Ford cars behind us on Main Street.

There's a second when Buzzy's eyes freeze to mine and that's when I know he ain't giving it up nohow. He takes a quick half step towards me like he's gonna try for the hedges, but then he jumps back the other way putting one of them Fords between hisself and McMullen.

Cursing, Mullen roars two shots into the windshield of the Ford Buzzy's ducked behind. The window crumbles and crashes all over the street. I drop to the ground, but I don't think none of them bullets get anywhere near to Buzzy, cause when I turn round he's still scuttling round the car. He's breathing hard and biting his lip like he's trying to work up the nerve to make for the hedges of one them frame house yards.

But McMullen firing them shots—it's like he give the high sign to every damn Cossack in town, cause the whole mess is headed up Main Street at a full gallop, guns drawn and sighted on Buzzy.

His pistol cinched out in front of hisself, McMullen heel-toes it towards the car that Buzzy's hiding behind. He lets go another shot into the fender to move Buzzy further around the car. Buzzy's trying like hell to keep that car between him and McMullen, but it don't matter nohow cause them horse Cossacks are closing in and there ain't a damn thing he can do.

"Give it up, boy!" McMullen says to him.

But Buzzy won't quit. He pushes off the car door and makes a dash up 8ᵗʰ Street, but it ain't no good. McMullen watches him run for the hedge fronting a house in the middle of the block. He rests his pistol on the top of his other arm and sights it in real careful. Then he cracks a shot straight into Buzzy's back.

I just sit there on the wood of the sidewalk and watch Buzzy fall. His body slaps down into the 8ᵗʰ Street dirt. McMullen and them other Cossacks all walk up and gather round. They kick at Buzzy a few times and then turn him over so they can get a look at his face.

Somebody says, "There's one dead pollock."

All of these bastards are laughing at my brother shot down like a dog.

I fly up off the sidewalk and dart over toward Buzzy. I'm shrieking and swinging my fists straight into the backs of them Pinkertons. I don't even feel it when they hit. Just bring 'em back and swing again.

I don't know how long I give it to them before somebody grabs hold of me from behind. I just feel hands on me, pulling me back, yanking my arms behind me. Then that goddamn McMullen is standing in front of me. Smiling. I'm screaming so loud I can't hear nothing but my own voice. It ain't even words coming outta my mouth. McMullen looks to the other Pinkertons and then points down to Buzzy with the high polished toe of his boot.

He smiles at me one more time before he pulls his fist back and crashes it into my face straight on. Then I'm on my behind in the dirt next to Buzzy. I'm crying so hard I can't even get no breath.

NINE

Telling my ma and Lottie, telling what happened to Buzzy, is plain, flat horrible. When I yank 'em outta bed, my ma tries to make a ruckus 'bout my eye being swolled shut. I can't even give that the time a day. I just pull both of 'em downstairs into the kitchen to get good away from Johnny and the twins before I say anything at all.

I try to be real strong like Buzzy was when I was a kid and he come home off the evening shift on the Marion seam. He wrapped his arm round my shoulder and set me down on the stoop to tell me about our pa getting killed down in the longwall cave-in with two other fellas. He told me we was going to have to look out for each other. But I can't make it. It ain't but two seconds after telling how they done for Buzzy that I'm hunched down at the kitchen table and gone to bawling.

My ma pulls at my arms, asking what happened, like she ain't heard nothing I told her. She just keeps asking the same questions over, like if she asks 'em enough times she'll get some different kind of answers. She grabs me tight and spins me round on the chair to face her. She keeps telling me, telling Lottie, that I must be wrong somehow. That there's some kinda mistake.

"I know yer brother wuz hard," she cries to me. "I know he wuz. But they wouldn't a kilt him. He was a boy."

I set there in the kitchen chair and I tell her that I wished I was wrong. That I wished I was a hundred percent wrong, but I seen Buzzy ducking behind that car, and I seen him making for that hedge. I heard them gunfire cracks and I touched the blood spread on the back of his wool coat. I tell her how I seen all of them bastard Pinkertons stand there laughing after they shot him down.

After I says that, my ma is backed up against the parlor door and screaming loud enough to drown out the tipple roar at high noon and I figure that I got to get hold of myself. That I can't be saying that stuff to my ma. I march out onto the porch and plop down onto the stoop. I watch the street for a while just looking at the moonlight shining crooked off the reddog pavement. I'm setting there trying to come to my senses like.

Lottie's really the only one of us who acts like she got some brains. She gets the lamp lit up and starts a pot of coffee on the coal stove. When my ma starts yelling to the whole neighborhood that she wants to see Buzzy's body, it's Lottie that takes her into the parlor and kneels her down in front of the crucifix.

My ma prays in Polish and she prays in English. Kneeling on the parlor rug, she's begging Saint Stanislaus to put in the word for Buzzy with Mary and with the Baby Jesus. She's weaving them rosary beads in her hands and cursing the Pinkertons too, but more than anything else, she's just crying, weeping like she ain't never gonna stop.

Later, Lottie pulls me back out onto the porch and takes a good look at my swelled up face. She asks me if I'm in trouble with the law too, but I just shake my head. I tell her them guards didn't seem to give two shits about me one way or the other. After, when I was lying there, they went walking back to their horses and McMullen went to his car. They sent for a man to get Buzzy's body up off the street. Then they talked 'bout going to get some beer from a bootlegger up in Scalp Level.

Lottie is really something. Setting down next to me, she takes my hand and tells me we're gonna be okay. She says to me that I shouldn't have had to see Buzzy get shot like that. We set there for a little while and then head back into the parlor and set with our ma on the sofa. When it gets towards light, my ma tucks herself into her print dress and slides her feet into her church shoes. We let Lottie to watch Johnny and the twins, and me and my ma head up to St. John's Church to see the Polish priest about a funeral for Buzzy.

Father Mizou don't need telling what happened. He says he seen the whole thing out the rectory window, so he knows why we come knocking on his door. He lets us in and puts his arms around my ma. She cries all sobbing like into his shoulder. He tells us to follow him into the rectory and we set down in the kitchen. Standing at the table, he takes a gander at the ridge around my eyes, swolled black and blue. He shakes his head and blows out a puff of air.

Father Mizou says for his housekeeper to give my ma some coffee, and he slips a little whiskey into the cup. I listen while they make a plan for Buzzy to get laid out up at our house today. Father Mizou says he'll call up the Miners' Lodge to send the funeral man and how our Lodge dues will pay the freight for Buzzy getting coffined up and hauled to the Polish Cemetery for burying.

My ma seems all right talking 'bout the wake and the graveyard plot and all. I mean she ain't screaming or fussing too much. But when it's time to go, she don't wanna head back out into the street. She has some more coffee and then Father Mizou wraps his arms around her again. On our way out the rectory door, he looks at my eye again and takes hold of my hand. He slides a quarter into my palm.

"Take care a yer mother, Chester," he says to me. "She's goin to have it rough."

I nod my head and drop the quarter in my pocket. We're all gonna have it rough, I wanna say. But Father Mizou's been nice, and I don't wanna be no kinda smart ass. So I walk down the steps and take hold of my ma's arm and walk with her on the plank sidewalk. I keep my body close to hers, so she can feel that somebody's there.

We walk like that the whole way through Windber. My ma ain't too steady on her feet and she has to stop every so often to blow her nose into the handkerchief she brung. While we're standing in front of La Monaca's Bakery, she takes a step back from me and firms up her face. She draws in a big breath, and she's wagging her finger in my chest and crying some.

"I know you're a good boy," she says to me. "But for all our sakes, ya gotta keep outta trouble now."

There's folks passing us on the sidewalk, but I'm looking right past 'em and past my ma talking at me. I'm staring back to the cross on the high spire of the Polish church. Standing there on the plank walk, I'm thinking about being in the rectory kitchen with Father Mizou, and I'm wondering if he'd a smiled at me and been so nice if he knew what we done to that dago fella up behind 40, if he knew what kind of man Buzzy really was.

When we get back to 40 Patchtown, we see Lottie's been real busy. She and Ol Lady Kosturko got all the ladies on Second Street to pitch in some kinda food for the wake. Ol Man Kosturko says he can get us a couple buckets of beer over in Paint. It means a lot, folks helping us out, cause I know they ain't got much their ownselfs.

I'm setting out on the porch when they horse wagon Buzzy's body up to our house. He's inside a pine coffin, and me and the funeral man and some of the fellas from the Miners' Lodge heave the coffin box into the parlor. We prop it up on the black sawhorses the funeral man brought, and I tell him to leave the lid down on the coffin till the priest gets here tonight. I don't want my ma or them young kids seeing Buzzy's body no more than they have to.

After we get the coffin fixed up and all, the funeral man heads back to Windber. He says he'll come back next morning to haul Buzzy off to the Polish boneyard up on Cemetery Ridge. I flop back down on the porch step waiting for Ol Man Kosturko to come back with them beers. Frankie comes out and sets hisself down next to me.

"Chester," he says to me. "Is it true that Buzzy's left us here to go to heaven?"

I look down at Frankie's bright blue eyes staring up at me and run the back of my hand cross my mouth and look away. I don't wanna show Frankie none of what's in my mind. Knowing what I know, I just can't say, "oh yeah, sure, kid." I just push my hand across the top of his head through his hair, blond and fine as cornsilk.

"Yer brother Buzzy loved ya a whole lot," is what I says to Frankie.

"So he's in heaven, right?"

"He loved me and ma and Lottie. He loved you and Esther and Johnny too."

After I says that, I spring up off the porch and leave Frankie holding his hat. I walk down to the end of Second Street to the school house where I ain't been for two years. I drop down on one of the wood board swings and just rock myself back and forth looking off at the high bony piles cross Paint Creek, trying to find some kind a way to make head or tail of the fix we're in.

I been setting there so long my hands are about froze when I see Charlie Dugan come trooping down Second Street. He's wearing an overcoat and a hat and he ain't smiling or nothing hiking down to the schoolyard. He comes over to where I'm setting and stands behind me. He puts his hand on my shoulder and says that he was down Windber and heard about what happened to Buzzy. He says that he come to offer his condolences.

"I hate 'em, Mr. Dugan," I says to him.

"I hate 'em, too, Chet," he says back to me. "I hate 'em too."

I set there for a minute or so thinking 'bout this. Then Mr. Dugan says that I can call him Charlie and he gives my shoulder a bit of a squeeze. I get up off of the swing and turn around to look him in the face.

"Someday we'll be free of all of these Cossacks," he says.

I don't say nothing to that, cause I just want Buzzy to come back and I don't really give two shits 'bout any of the rest of this right now.

"C'mon, Chet," Charlie says. "Let's go up to the house. See if your ma needs anything."

So I go walking with Charlie back up to our house and there's all kinda people there now. A lotta men from the union brung beer, and some brang wine. They're standing round the kitchen talking 'bout the strike and cursing the Berwinds. Some men are talking about how they got Buzzy, some are talking about what happened down the train station, most are saying we oughtta lynch that bastard McMullen. The men in the kitchen are saying about how my eye is yellowing up and swolled near to shut. A few says they're sorry about that too. I just nod and try not to start crying in front of any of them.

Them union men's wives is there too and they brung pigs in a blanket and pierogies. There's halushki too and blueberry blintzes for sweet.

I find my ma in the parlor slumped in the chair in front of Buzzy's coffin. Most all of the *studda babas* from 40 are either setting in the parlor or standing round behind her.

Them old ladies are all drinking coffee, saying the rosary of the sorrowful mysteries.

Lottie's running round pouring coffee for some of them *studda babas* and the twins is both on the parlor floor setting next to ma. Ma is praying and she's crying some every so often, but nothing like before. I set with them in the parlor for a couple Hail Marys, then I go back out to the kitchen to be with the union men while we all wait for the Polish priest.

I've got down some of them pierogies, and I'm having a little of the whiskey somebody brung from over Third Street when Charlie Dugan comes over to me. He says that he gotta head back up to Cresson on the union's business. He tells me again how he's real sorry 'bout what happened to Buzzy. Then he says if there's anything I need, I should talk to him direct.

I says thanks to him for that and I ask him if he wants to take anything to eat with him. He says he's all right and we go out on the porch where some men are smoking cigarettes. Standing there, we shake hands like men before Charlie starts down the sidewalk and heads across the street to get in his Ford.

When he drives off, I go back into the kitchen and Father Mizou comes a couple minutes later. Everybody puts down their plates and all the glasses of beer and we all shuffle into the parlor. The funeral man and Father Mizou lift the lid off of Buzzy's casket. The funeral man changed Buzzy's clothes, so you can't see he was shot down, but his face is awful white. I take a good, long look at Buzzy's face, trying to get it burnt into my mind, so I don't never forget it, but it ain't even been one day and he don't look nothing like he did alive. So I just say forget it and stand with Lottie behind our ma who's setting up next to the foot of the casket.

All the people, the union men and their wives and the *studda babas* gather round behind us and Father Mizou stands up by Buzzy's head. He reads from the missal 'bout how Buzzy's gonna rise up with the Lord Jesus in the last days. I want him to rise up now, but I ain't saying nothing. Lottie snatches hold of the twins and puts them back away with Johnny in the kitchen when they start screaming and carrying on. Ol Man Kosturko and his wife are crying some. But off to the side of the casket, my ma really starts to break down again. Weeping full on, she looks like somebody stole all the bones right outta her face.

The next morning, we haul Buzzy off to the Polish Cemetery in the Miners' Lodge horse wagon. Lots of folks from all over 40 and some from other patchtowns and even some from Windber come up for the burying. Father Mizou gives Buzzy the dust to dust and then my ma and me and Lottie and the twins and Johnny all toss a handful of dirt down on Buzzy's casket. Then some Miners' Lodge fellas lower Buzzy into the ground and all the *studda babas* dirge out the *Anioł Pański* which is the Polish funeral song and the saddest song in the world.

After they're done, me and Lottie grab up my ma's hands and take hold of the other kids. With everybody walking behind us, we hoof it slow down the curve of the Ridge Road back to 40 with nobody saying nothing.

Ten

The Cossacks only wait a week to come calling, till the union men and all our neighbors are gone away from our house back to their own troubles. That's when the sunsabitches march up, eviction papers crumpled in their dirty mitts. The first two Pinkertons stomping up the walk, big-bellied and stinking of corn liquor, they're strange to me. But the older one trailing up behind, I recognize right off. His name is Coulson and he's blond-headed and lanky with his lip is curled up funny so his long, flat face always looks like he just pissed his pants. More than once since this strike started up, I spied him huddled with Buzzy in the alleyway behind the 40 Hotel when they thought nobody was looking.

That first Cossack, he shoves them eviction papers under my nose and pushes right past me onto the screen porch like I'm standing on the porch of *his* house. Hollerin like a teacher who been wanting to kick you outta the oneroom all year long and finally got the go-ahead, he tells me since Buzzy's dead we gotta shag our pollock asses outta the company's house. I tell him that I'm a loader on the B seam at 40 mine, so we can stay on that. But he won't go for it nohow. He says he don't give St. Peter's pecker if I'm superintendent of Eureka 37, we gotta hit the road.

"Make yourself some pollock tracks, little pollock," he yells at me.

Then he twists the screen door off the hinges and stomps right into our house. He's rampaging through the kitchen,

He's yelling, "Younz got till dark to get your pollock shit the hell out a here."

Both the other Pinkerton and Coulson start in after him, but I snatch hold of Coulson's blue dye coat and give it a tug.

"Ain't there nothin you can do?" I ask him. "Ya know my brother just got shot."

"Younz is lucky ya got to stay on this long," he says soft.

"We pay our rent," I tell him.

"Ya paid more than that."

"How ya mean?"

Coulson pulls me over to the corner of the porch and says low to me that's the deal they had going with Buzzy. Them other Cossacks didn't like him none, but ten dollars every month put on top of the ten dollar rent and they let us stick. Now I understand how come I kept seein him sneaking round with Buzzy the beginning of every month.

"Shit," he says. "'Thout that sugar money younz woulda been throwed outta here six months ago like every other trouble maker."

"What if I can get you the money?" I ask him.

"Too late now," he says. "With Buzzy bein in a shootout and all, McMullen would cut my throat he knew you was stayin on in a company house."

I'm 'bout ready to tell him that Buzzy wasn't in no shootout. He just got shot. But I hear my sister yelling all high-pitched from upstairs. She's screaming for them Cossacks to keep away from her. So, I leave that damn Coulson holding his hat and go running into the house. I grab my ma's big sewing shears off the darning bench in the parlor and take them wood stairs two at a time.

I find them all in the back bedroom. Them bastards got Lottie pushed back into the corner of the room next to the clothes cabinet. She's cursing and holding 'em off with a dressing table chair stuck out in front of her.

I grab a water pitcher off the dresser top and throw it up against the wall. It shatters, spraying shiny square pieces of glass cross the bedroom floor. Both of them Pinkertons look at me like they're gonna tear me in two.

"Get outta here, boy!" they tell me. "Get your dumb ass back downstairs."

But my blood's up and I just don't care what happens. I flip the sewing shears open and hold them out in front of me. I try to spread my weight over both feet like I seen Buzzy do in a knife fight with a fella from out 42.

"I ain't got nothing to lose," I tell them Cossacks. "Younz better scram on outta here or kill me right here and now. I'll find ya whereever ya go. Kill ya both, if I have to set fire to ya while ya sleep."

The look on their faces changes, and I wonder if I'm looking just crazy enough to scare 'em off. Then I look closer and see that they're looking behind me, over my head. That Cossack Coulson's standing in the doorway. He's got his hands on his hips and he's shaking his head.

"I ain't gonna let this happen here," he says. "We come down here to throw these pollocks out and we'll do it. But younz fool with that girl, I'll fix ya my own damn self."

The two Cossacks start trying to argue him into going along, but this Coulson ain't having none of it. He throws his coat open and shows 'em the chrome steel pistol parked in his dark, polished holster. They look at each other like they're trying to figure whether to shit or go blind. I'm still standing there waving the sewing shears out in front of me and watching Lottie, who's let the chair drop 'bout halfway to the floor.

When Coulson lowers his hand to the pearl butt of that pistol, them other two Pinkertons look at him like he's lost his mind.

"Bobby Coulson," one of them says. "Ya mean to tell me you'd shoot down yer own kind for these pollocks?"

"What we're doin here," Coulson says slow, almost tired like, "throwin these pollocks in the street, might not be right. But I got two kids to feed. So, if it ain't right, so be it. But what ya wanna do to that girl's just plain wrong. I'll tell the both of you right now, I ain't goin to hell just so ya can get a piece a Polish ass."

The whole time Coulson's been saying this, his hand's been slowly wrapping itself around that pistol butt. When them bastards hear the click from his thumb snapping the holster tab open, it seems to settle the matter for everybody. They step back away from Lottie and she lowers the chair the rest of the way to the floor. I move off to the side of the door frame so them sunsabitches can get clear of the room without getting too near to me, just in case beating my ass ain't a hell causing kinda sin.

"Thank you, mister," I says to Coulson when the other Cossacks have gone down the hallway.

"Don't ya thank him," Lottie says. "He didn't do nothin for us. It's his soul he's worried about."

"She's right," Coulson almost spits at me. "I didn't do nothin for ya. So ya make sure ya got all of yer pollock shit outta here before dark."

Now, I don't understand how Lottie could say he didn't do nothing for her. If he hadn't a stepped up, she might be getting it from them Cossacks this minute instead of standing here talking, but now Coulson just seems to want us to get our stuff and get the hell out, so I don't know.

When Coulson and them other Cossacks is gone, I says to Lottie that we best tell our ma 'bout getting the boot out.

But Lottie's setting down over by the clothes closet in the chair she was fending them Cossacks off with. She's got her hand on her forehead and she's just staring into the wall looking played out and I'm thinking maybe the business with them Cossacks took more outta her than she wants to let on.

I tell her it's all right, that she can just sit there for a while and I'll go tell our ma about the papers. She don't say nothin, just keeps looking blank at the paint peeling wall of the back bedroom.

My ma is at the neighbor's down on First Street cross from the pick-me store. She got the twins and Johnny with her and the neighbor must have give 'em some kinda sugar candy for a bribe cause they're all keeping quiet for once. I come up on them setting on the porch to hear my ma telling the neighbor lady 'bout how hard it's been not having no husband for so long and how maybe if my pa hadn't gotten killed down West Virginia, Buzzy might a turned out different. She sounds to be damn near crying, saying 'bout how she can't hardly stand this no more.

She can't see me cause the porch is built up high on cinder blocks, and I'm skulking down by the coal chute underneath. I give her a second to quiet down before I pop up them steps. When I do clomp up, I make it good and loud, so she'll know I'm coming.

"Hey ma," I says to her.

"Chester," she says back. When she sees me, she's still breathy and weepy in her talk, but she tries to say my name all regular, like she's not that sad at all.

"I know ya don't need no more of it," I says to her, "but I got some bad news."

My ma looks at me with her mouth flopped open while I tell her 'bout getting served up the papers. I don't say nothing 'bout what happened with Lottie and the Cossacks. I figure if my ma's already had too much to take, learning 'bout that on top of us getting throwed out might just send her round the bend.

Now, my ma knows they only give ya till dark to get your stuff outta them company houses when ya get served up papers, but she ain't getting up or nothing. I grab hold of her arm and give her a heave, but like I said before, my ma's a big woman and she don't go nowhere till I look over for the neighbor lady to say something.

"Anna," she says to my ma. "Ya gotta get home and pack what ya can get out or them Cossacks is gonna get all your stuff."

My ma snuffles out she don't care 'bout who gets nothing. She says she don't even know where we'll go. But then maybe she figures out she sounds like a little kid saying she don't care who gets our stuff or maybe she realizes that we're gonna go down to Tent City like everybody else in 40 what got their stuff set out, I don't know. But after a second, she gets up and pulls her dress straight. She grabs Johnny's hand and tells me, "Chester, lay hold of them sticky twins. We gotta pack."

Eleven

While my ma and Lottie are trying their best to get what they can of our stuff packed up, I head up to McKluskey's farm with Ol Man Kosturko to borrow their wagon.

Them McKluskeys must feel bad 'bout us getting the boot out so quick after Buzzy being shot down cause they don't even ask for no money to use the horse wagon. The oldest of the McKluskey boys just says to make sure to have it back to them before dark.

Ol Man Kosturko and me bounce on the buckboard of the wagon down Patchtown Road past Eureka 40 to Ash Alley where we jerk a right up onto Second Street. When we draw even with my house, Stash and Baldy are setting on the porch on top of some packed up freight boxes. Stash says to me they're sorry they didn't come up to the house for Buzzy's laying out.

"We was scared to even show up at the buryin," Stash says. "We didn't know if them Pinkertons was gonna be waiting up there at the cemetery for us."

"Ya know, hiding behind tombstones," Baldy says.

I give a look to Ol Man Kosturko and he goes in the house to help my ma. Then I says to Baldy and Stash that I don't think them Pinkertons ever found out about nobody beside Buzzy. I tell 'em that them bastards coulda had me dead to rights, they'd a wanted. But they just let me lay.

"Whatcha think happened?" Baldy asks me. "How'd they find out?"

I know I ain't seen Mikey since that day I stomped out of the 40 Hotel. I don't think he would a give Buzzy up outright even for money, but I can see him letting something slip trying to make up for his not being down at the 40 station riot. But I don't know that for sure neither, so I just shrug my shoulders like I can't figure nothing.

Baldy and Stash both gimme a nod, but I can see they don't believe I'm giving them a hundred percent of the truth. For a second, they look at me like maybe it was me that said something. But they must realize I wouldn't rat out my own brother nohow, because they don't say nothing else about it. Maybe they're thinking about Mikey being gone too.

It don't take too long to load what we got up into the back of the wagon cause Stash and Baldy give us a hand heaving them boxes. Besides, my ma knows we can only take so much to the Tent City. She gives some of our stuff to the Kosturkos and she sells the couple pieces of furniture we got to some Slovaks living over on Third Street.

We make sure we get all of our clothes and dishes and pots and stuff like that loaded up onto the wagon before it's even close to dark, cause them Cossacks come and nail your door shut the night they serve papers and whatever they find in your house after that they keep for theirselfs. Right before we roll the wagon out, Baldy and Stash tell me that they gotta get a move on back over the rock dump to 37 Patchtown. They're acting like they're still afraid of getting seen by them Pinkertons, but since Buzzy got shot down, the curfew's lightened up a good bit it seems to me. So maybe they're still spooked a little, but I wonder if it ain't that they was Buzzy's friends more than they ever was mine and just don't want to be running with nobody who aint' yet turned fifteen.

"Okay, fellas," I tell 'em. "I'll see ya around."

Stash and Baldy start back through the yards towards Paint Creek and with the wagon balanced up with our stuff, we head off down Patchtown Road for the Tent Camp on the other side of the 40 Hotel.

What folks call the Tent City is a camp of tents and chicken coops built up in the patch of scrub woods behind the 40 Hotel on land that belongs to one of the McKluskey brothers. He lives somewhere in Ohio, so he don't gotta be 'fraid of the Berwinds giving it to him for letting the miners set up on his land. Since this strike started, it's maybe half of 40 that's got the boot out, but there ain't that many left livin down in the Tent City. A lot, I think, went maybe to Pittsburgh to try for steel mill work and some headed back east to load in the anthracite mines. More than a few just drifted the hell away.

When I get the horse wagon off of Patchtown Road and take her up the Tent City Trail through the woods, all the people what's there look up to see who's coming in now. I recognize some fellas from the union meetings and I see a good many folks what lived down 40 before the strike, but ain't been back on account of all the Pinkertons knocking heads. Some folks are pointing at me or waving cause they know I'm Buzzy's brother or they recognize me from the B seam washhouse, but it seems everybody's deep enough in their own troubles that they ain't in no mood to be getting up and running over to give me a proper handshake.

Spread through the trees, the Tent City is maybe thirty some tents and a bunch of festering coops and some lean-to's built out of barn boards. Kids and women set on oak logs around a big cook fire burning in the center of the camp. Every one of them setting looks pretty glum, and none of the ones standing looks much better.

I was thinking it might be tough to get a tent spot down here, but with all the folks that's left or been run off, there's a good many places already been cleared out of brush and the like, so we head over to one of them patches on the outskirts away from the smoke of the cookfire. I says to my ma that her and Lottie and Esther oughtta get to unloading our stuff off the wagon while I take Frankie with me to find the head union man so we can see 'bout getting us a tent.

Walking back through the rough clutter of that tent camp sets me to thinking. I figured that we really had it bad down 40. But some of these folks in Tent City has been here since the beginning of the strike back in April and they look like they're gonna be lucky just to make the morning. I ain't lying. I mean kids is looking at Frankie all jealous and pointing, whispering behind their hands, and at first I can't figure out why. But then I see these little kids ain't got no kinda shoes. They're walking around the rain puddles and the brambles with nothin but old strips of pit britches wrapped round their feet.

I feel bad about seeing their feet all cut to hamburger meat, but just the same I take hold of Frankie's thin shoulder and pull him over close to me.

I cup a whisper in his ear. "Frankie," I tell him. "No matter what happens in this here camp, ya make sure to keep a good eye on yer brogans."

The head union man for the camp is Lefty Jankowsky's brother Stiney, but one of them sad fellas loafing round the cook fire says he ain't due to come back till later tonight, so me and Frankie drop down onto one of them logs to wait.

Setting there round the fire with Frankie, I give them Tent City folks a second look and I recognize more and more of them. The Stankevichs what used to live over Third Street and the Kietas from the top of Ash Alley and maybe half them Marcinkos from down Third Street, they're all camped out in the couple of wartime tents with one cow and probably two dozen thin kids between 'em. When I'm scouring faces back away from the side of the fire, looking for some of the trapper boys I used to know from 40 mine, I spy out one of the girls I seen down at the platform during the 40 station riot.

She's stomping outta one of the lean-to's wearing a house dress that must be her ma's, cause it hangs off her like a pair of curtains. Her hair's white blond and straight as a ruler. She's maybe an inch taller than me with full lips. Her eyes are ice water blue, set in a hard kind of way like Buzzy's. She's carrying a coffee pot full of water, and she pushes folks outta her way to get up close to the cook fire.

"Hey there," I says to her. "I'm Chet and this here is my brother Frankie. We just got here today."

"Hey yerself, trapper boy" she scowls. "I know who ya are."

Even scowling like a pitboss, she's the prettiest girl I ever seen. I watch her rake a bed of coals level and set her coffee pot down in the corner of the cook fire. When she gets it fixed in there pretty good, she backs up and sets down on the log across the fire from Frankie. She crosses her legs under that big ol dress and looks off into the trees.

"It was yer brother got shot out in front of the Polish church by the Pinkerton boss," she says to me.

"McMullen," I says. "That was the bastard shot him down."

"Fella like yer brother," she says. "Wuz only a matter a time 'fore somebody did."

I spring up off of my log, and pretty girl or no, I'm getting ready to take a poke and set her straight. But her pa comes hoofing it over from the other side of the fire. He's big as a draft horse with a voice to match. He yells at her to apologize for saying that to me.

"He can go to hell," she tells her pa. "You can slide along right behind him if ya think that any Pistakowski's gonna be getting an apology off the likes of me."

I can't believe that this girl is talking to her pa like that. Then I watch her snatch up the coffee pot quick as lightning and for a second, I think I'm gonna get a face full. But she just makes a show of dropping it straight onto the ground, then stomps off back to the lean-to she come outta before.

"I'm sorry 'bout what happened to yer brother," her pa says to me after we set there for a minute.

He picks the coffee pot up outta the dirt and gives it a little dustoff.

I grab Frankie by the hand to start back to where our ma's unloading the wagon, but this girl's pa is an awful big fella. He takes a steady grip on my shoulder, holding me so I can't go nowhere.

"Pauline's Aunt Sis was one of them got trampled down the 40 station rushing to get clear of the Pinkertons. Pauline watched her get both her arms broke," he says. "I believe Pauline holds Buzzy some at fault."

"My brother's dead."

"I know he is," he says to me. "And that ain't right either."

Pauline's pa stands there for a long minute before he goes on, like he's figuring whether to say any more. Finally, he says, "I know it's hard, but you gotta understand a lotta people knew what yer brother was like. The things he done. It ain't easy to let go of that. For a lot of folks, the trouble-makers on our side ain't much less to blame for what's happening than the guards theirselves."

When he's done talking, he eases up on me so I can walk off if I like. But I stand my ground. I let go of Frankie's hand and turn and look up his thick chest and broad shoulders and heavy neck, straight up into in his eye. I look at him close and serious and trying to make it sound as much man to man as I can, I tell him that it's a pity what happened to folks down the station.

"A damn shame," I says. "I'm sorry for any part Buzzy had to do with it."

Pauline's pa yanks the lid off the coffee pot and gives it a little sniff. For a second, he looks off into the thinned out stand of trees, staring like maybe he's seeing something I can't, something that ain't even there. He shakes his head and says to me that he knows who's liable for what went on down the station.

"Them Pinkertons," he says, "they planned to give it to us whether or not Buzzy was even there."

There's a funny little moment of quiet and then Pauline's pa sticks out his big hand. He tells me that his name is Mr. Paul Obanek and asks me if I wanna have some of his coffee. I let him give my hand a pump with that big calloused mitt of his and say okay. He gets me a blue tinwork miner's cup outta his lean-to. He pours me a dose and we set down on the log on the other side of the fire to get outta the smoke cause the wind's changed and now it's blowing in from the other way.

I ask Mr. Paul how long he been in this Tent City and he says they been camped since right after the strike got started up. He spins it out for me how he used to be fire boss out Eureka 35, but when the union started coming around signing fellas up, he didn't call them out and so the seam boss kicked him back down to loader. When the strike come down he was one of the first to get served up his papers. Him and Pauline camped out in the 35 copses for a bit with some other fellas, but couldn't find no place down there them Pinkertons wouldn't come riding through at night looking to pull down their tents and threaten to cart them off to the jailhouse.

Hearing all this, I'm fair impressed, cause being fire boss is a big-time job. A man gotta know a damn lot to be fire boss anywhere and Eureka 35 ain't no penny ante mine. I'm real curious to listen to what Mr. Paul's got to say about making it as a miner.

We set there jawing for a good while, Mr. Paul and me. I like the way he talks to me like I'm a grown man and not some aged-up trapper boy. We talk about how to judge the right amount of powder for blasting the coal chucks off the rock face and not blowing the coal into dust.

"Even we get this new contract," he says. "Loading's always gonna put more silver in a fella's pocket than mucking around with that deadwork."

He also jokes with me about keeping a close eye on the tippleman, so he don't shave no weight on my coal. We keep on like this, till we get to trying to figure what suffering this strike is gonna get us from these damn operators. That's when people start yelling that Stiney Jankowsky's making his way back to the Tent City.

Stiney comes galloping quick through the dim woods into the tent camp on a big sorrel mare, leaping over downed trees and rocks. All wound up, he flops himself down off that horse and goes sprinting round the whole camp whispering something to each of the miners, rousting 'em outta their tents and yanking 'em outta their coops.

I trail round after Stiney trying to get his attention, but he's got a list of names he's reading from and won't gimme the time of day. Finally, I grab onto the sleeve of his coat. I says to him that I'm a miner too and anything he got to say to these other fellas he can damn well say to me.

At first he don't know who I am, but when Mr. Paul tells him that I'm Buzzy Pistakowski's brother, Stiney Jankowsky shakes my hand. He gives a long look at the yellowing round my eye and waggles his head.

"I'm sorry," Stiney says, "bout the way them Cossacks done Buzzy."

Then he pulls me off to the side of one of them pine board chicken coops. He looks around a second to see if anybody's listening before he lets me in on what he's telling. Charlie Dugan's on his way back from Cresson tonight and the union's declared an emergency meeting. All the union miners are getting together out Gerula's farm at nine o'clock.

I run back over to the cook fire and find Frankie. I tell him to let our ma know that her and Lottie's gonna need to take the wagon back up to McKluskey's when it's unloaded cause I gotta head up Ashtola tonight on important union business.

TWELVE

Hoofing it over the narrow dirt path that winds up through the high brown weeds of Meckley's Field, my eyes are fixed to the bouncing yellow glow from Mr. Paul's carbide, but my mind is running circles round itself trying to take in all that's happened today.

Not that the eviction ain't pressing on my mind—it ain't gonna be no picnic down that tent camp—but mostly I'm thinking 'bout that twitch-faced Coulson and how he run them other Cossacks off of messing with Lottie. Lottie thought he ought to go to hell and just about said as much to him. And it's true he's with the Pinkertons, so he can't be no kinda all right fella. But on the other hand, I know I ain't wrong that if he wouldn't a been there, we'd a been worse for it. I just can't figure it, 'cept I guess that even among folks that mean to do ya harm, some fellas is worse than others.

It's a pretty good walk up to Gerula's and nobody's saying nothing. So, I got plenty of time for thinking—and that Pauline's on my mind too, specially the way that expression on her face was like to remind me of Buzzy. But not like Buzzy at the same time. I mean Buzzy would give a fella a beating just to see somebody get one. Ol Pauline might need a reason, but she don't seem to be above turning over a rock or two to find one.

It's all got me thinking 'bout the riot down the train station and how even though Buzzy was one of the people causing a good bit of the trouble, it didn't mean nothing to him when it was over, 'cept some guards getting paid out with a slingshot or broom handle. But for folks like Pauline's aunt, her whole life was caught up in it.

It's like tossing a rock into the Paint Creek swimming hole. Even if you turn away after you throw the rock and don't watch, the ripples is still there. Like what Buzzy done helped to make Pauline the way she is. Maybe we all help to make each other the way we are. I don't know.

When Mr. Paul and me top the rise and start down into Gerula's orchard, I can see right off there's a lot fewer fellas at this meeting than at the last one. Mr. Paul tries to tell me it's cause the union's afraid that the Berwinds been sending spies to our meetings, but looking at these fellas, it seems to me there's more to it than that.

Most of the miners who got to the meeting before us is setting on a sloping hill in a big half circle under the trees closest to Gerula's horse barn. Me and Mr. Paul head over to join them. Up close, I can see they're all looking skeleton thin, and their eyes got dark circles like they're still working double shifts. Patched up with shreds of pit vest and rawhide, their shoes don't look much better than what the boys are using to pad around down the Tent City. Even the men what ain't been put out look pretty downhearted, grumbling 'bout how long we been on strike and doubting that we're gonna get anything for all our troubles. To listen to some of the fellas, I get the feeling that they might be getting ready to call it quits. They're saying that a lotta miners up north already went back to work and with that coal coming outta them mines we ain't never gonna get Berwind to give us our due. It ain't that I don't see their point, but there ain't no way I'm ready to give it up yet.

When I see Charlie Dugan pull up on the other side of the orchard in his black Ford, I'm about to run over there to say hey to him. But all kinds of fancy fellas that I ain't never seen before come outta his car. Every one of them got hats and neckties and there's one big fella that seems to be keeping everybody else pretty good away from Charlie. So I just settle for trading waves.

"You a friend a Charlie D?" Mr. Paul asks me.

I figure he might wanna talk, so we don't have to listen to the fellas setting in front of us pissing and moaning, so I start telling Mr. Paul how Charlie saved my *dupa* down the 40 station. I'm only part way through my story 'fore I realize what happened to his sister down that train station massacre ain't gonna be no kinda topic he wants to hear about. So I switch to telling him 'bout Charlie running the union store up 42. I let it slip that Buzzy didn't care none for Charlie, but Mr. Paul don't make nothing of this. He listens good and before I know it, I done told him the whole story 'bout what happened in 42 with Buzzy's stealing them pears outta the union tent and what come after.

His face creases and his brown eyes go flat sad taking it in, then Mr. Paul nods to me and gives me a little slap across my shoulder. We both turn and see that Charlie Dugan's started walking over from his car to the front of the crescent of grumbling miners. Some of his boys has come over, and they're telling everybody to pipe down cause the meeting's coming to order. But a lotta folks is still talking 'tween their selfs, griping and kicking the union ain't doing nothing for 'em.

Even when Charlie hisself gets up to the front of the crowd, some of them miners won't quiet down. Every time he says something, some smart ass starts putting his two cents in, pissing and moaning 'bout how hard things is and how they ain't making no money. Some fellas are even talking about the organizers getting rich on the union dues.

Charlie tries to answer all these bullshitters in turn, but I can see that there's really only two or three that's egging on the rest. I push myself up off the ground and start toward the front of the meeting. Mr. Paul grabs my coat sleeve, but I shake loose of him and make my way through the crowd up to the front of the miners.

"Listen to me!" I says standing up in front of the whole group of them miners. "We been fightin these Berwinds now for goin on eight damn months. I know it's hard. My own brother's been shot. My family been put out. I know I ain't alone. I know a lot a younz here tonight are livin in the tents and coops, living in sheds. But don't ya be blamin Charlie. He been a damn good leader to us since he come down here."

One of them ol bullshitters setting up in front of where me and Mr. Paul was starts up yelling that I'm ain't even a real miner.

"Sit down, ya trapper boy," he says. "Come back when ya got some hair on your sack."

I can feel the crowd is starting to laugh with him and that's when I realize that I'm standing up here, in front of everybody, me, Chester Pistakowski, trying to tell all the miners of Windber that I know what's what better than they do. But I also recognize that the fella yelling at me is that same skinny Grubby Koshinsky who was hollering the loudest down the 40 station when them Pinkerton guards was cornered up on the mantrip car.

"You was pretty hot for this coal strike back at the 40 station," I says to him. "Talkin 'bout how you was gonna be givin scabs the beat down and the Cossacks too. What's a matter now, Grubby, yer balls only work when the sun shines?"

Everybody laughs at that, and Grubby's friends are ribbing him pretty good for taking that kinda shit off of some kid. He pushes hisself up off of the ground like to come after me and I figure I'm gonna get a hiding, but before he gets the whole way up, Mr. Paul yanks him back onto the chilly ground by the tail of his coat. He crashes down onto the ground and everybody gets a good laugh outta that, saying he's been one too many times to the bootleggers.

Lucky for me, Charlie steps back out in front of the meeting with two of them other fellas he brung down from Cresson. He starts in on everybody, asking them if they wanna have a meeting or a brawl. After a little bit more shouting most everybody quiets the hell down so Charlie can talk.

"I know ya boys are gettin frustrated! I know yer tired! Tired a losin to the Berwinds," Charlie says. "Tired a them shootin ya down in the streets. Tired a them puttin ya outta yer houses. And I damn sure know yer tired a seein yer kids hungry!"

Charlie's a real good talker, and pretty soon he's got most everybody setting in that field remembering that it's the Berwinds we're actually fighting against. I watch him close and outta the corner of his mouth he seems to be smiling at me for taking his side. But I can also see that Grubby is looking at me too and that he ain't about to forget no time soon the way I made him out an ass tonight.

When Charlie gets done with his pep talk, he fixes his hat and clears his throat. He says that the head union men up in Cresson has decided it's time we oughtta try some new strategy on the Berwinds.

"We're takin the fight right to EJ Berwind's front door!" he says.

Nobody really says nothing, till Charlie explains that instead of all of us standing on the picket line down here in Windber where nobody can see us, the Mine Workers Union is gonna send a passel of men to picket in Philadelphia. Charlie tells us that old Berwind won't be able to walk past his own office without seeing ten men decked out in full miners' clothes right on Broad Street.

"Let him try to hold his head high for his fancy friends with starving men right outside his front door," Charlie says. "He won't be pretendin he ain't got no labor troubles then!"

I'm smirking along with everybody else picturing a pack of miners picketing in front of Berwind's fancy office tucked into pit vests, carbide lamps topping their heads and toting picks and shovels. Seems to me this is the first time a lotta these men was happy about anything for a damn long time.

"That'll get the bastard to settle," some fellas are saying.

We all cheer and raise a ruckus and people start offering to go cross state to do the picketing. In the end there's so many volunteers to go that Charlie's gotta pick 'em by lottery.

I step back away from everybody while Charlie draws names outta his hat. I'm watching the whole bunch of us laughing and it feels okay, but I can't laugh too hard, cause I can't quite shake hearing Buzzy laugh his mean old laugh and saying how we was gonna get them bastards one way or another. And looking round, I see that even though Mr. Paul done put his name in to go over Philadelphia and picket, he ain't laughing so much neither.

THIRTEEN

It ain't till the next morning that we finally get our tent from the union. Two scruffy fellas I ain't never seen before heave it off the back of a horse wagon onto the scrubby patch of ground Lottie and the twins cleared out of rocks and sticks. I shout up to them if they'll help us to get the thing set up, but they're already jockeying the wagon back through the woods out to Patchtown Road.

I get Lottie and Frankie to give me a hand with driving the stakes into the dirt and Mr. Paul comes over and pitches in with the poles, so it don't take too long before we got the damn thing raised up. It's leaning some off to the left and Esther's saying it smells like a diaper that nobody bothered to wash, but after a night sleeping in the open, I don't think none of us care two bits.

Once we get all the pots and blankets and whatnot we brung from Second Street stacked inside the tent, my ma hands the twins a couple gallon buckets and shoos them out into the woods to gather up acorns. She tells Lottie and me we're gonna have to be eating black acorn mush for a bit. She says we oughtta make out that we like it in front of the twins and Johnny, no matter what it tastes like. Lottie just groans she didn't sleep worth a damn last night out in the damp air and she's going in the tent to get some proper rest.

I don't know nothing 'bout making no black acorn mush and I ain't too keen on learning, so I wander over to the cook fire. It's still a little cold from last night and more than a couple folks are setting round warming theirselfs off the flames licking up out of the fire pit.

I says "hey" to everybody and set my ass down on one of the logs put round the fire. Some folks is roasting up corn ears at the edge of the fire in the bed of red glowing coals. Cooking through them husks, that corn smells like pretty good breakfast to me and I ask them folks setting around where they got it.

One of them Slovak girls, what used to run with Buzzy, clues me in they been picking for the farmers out in Ashtola. She says they been dragging theirselves out there every morning and them kraut farmers put 'em to work in the fields bringing in the potato crop. The farmers mostly let 'em take a half bushel of potatoes for a day of picking. Sometimes they even get a few corn ears or maybe a bit of milk or eggs to boot.

She turns them corn cobs over in the fire and I tell her that sounds all right to me. I says to her about how we got our stuff set out by the Pinkertons and ain't got much of nothing left to eat.

I say that even with what happened to Buzzy, I still got two brothers and a older sister. I tell her that Lottie and me is real good workers and even though my other brothers and sister is young they can work hard too. But before I can ask her how we can get on picking with one of them farmers, she's already starting to look off in the other direction, like she don't wanna hear the rest of what I got to say.

"What's a matter?" I ask her. "Won't them krauts hire on no pollocks?"

"If them kraut farmers stopped hirin pollocks," another woman says to me, "they'd have a hell of a time gettin them damn potatoes picked at all."

"So how come they wouldn't want to hire me on?"
I ask. "I can load coal on the B seam I can damn sure pick
potatoes!"

I got no choice but to listen to that green wood
crackling away in the cook fire for a minute, cause none of
them women are saying nothing. I can feel the damp rising
up off the log bark and getting into the seat of my pants. I
stand up and step over to where the fire's hotter. I don't say
nothing, just stand there with my ass turned towards the flames
steaming the damp outta my britches.

Finally, one of the other women, a Slovak what used
to live down First Street, says to me that all of them farmers
are about done with their harvests. She says I should have been
here two, three weeks back. There was plenty of work then,
potatoes, apples, even pears, she says. But most all of them
crops has been put up by now.

I don't feel there's nothing to say to them after that,
so I just set back down next to the fire and wait for the twins
to come scurrying back with the acorn buckets. The girl that
knowed Buzzy must feel bad seeing me all down in the dumps
about the way things are shaking out, cause when I get up she
gives me a half dozen corn ears and a couple potatoes to take
back to our tent.

My ma perks up a bit when she sees I brung a spot
of food over. She divides all the stuff up and puts it on the
dinner plates we brung from our house. When the twins get
back, my ma takes the acorns they hunted up and dumps 'em
into a wash tub of water to leech out the poison. Then she has
us all set down on some rocks next to our tent to eat. We're all
pretty damn hungry and them corn ears go awful quick and the
potatoes don't last much longer.

When Esther and Frankie start asking how come we
got these big old plates and hardly no food, Lottie tells them
to hush. But they ain't having it, neither of them. They're both

whining and carrying on, saying how they wanna eat pierogies and halushki and have blintzes for dessert.

"Ya kids oughtta be thankful ya got food to eat," Lottie says to them. "There's plenty kids round here be damn glad to have what ya got."

"My ass, Lottie," Frankie says.

I look over at Lottie cause I'm hoping she's gonna let Frankie slide on account of all that's going on, but no chance. She's already up off her butt ready to whack him right cross his gob when Mr. Paul comes hoofing past our tent.

"Charlotte," he says to my sister. "If you got time to cook 'em, me and Pauline got some cabbages over here that we ain't got no use for."

My sister tries to tell him that we're doing okay, that we don't need no help, but Mr. Paul won't take no for an answer—which is good, cause if Lottie actually kept Mr. Paul from giving us them cabbages to eat, I think me and Frankie both would like to have drown her in the middle of Paint Creek.

After Lottie lets up, Mr. Paul brings both Pauline and them cabbages over. They set down next to us on the rocks and my ma starts tearing up one of them cabbage heads. Frankie and Esther set there watching her, making sure, I guess, she don't drop none of them leaves on the ground. Lottie uses a corner of her dress to wipe a smear of potato from round Johnny's mouth.

Mr. Paul says that Pauline overheard me talking to them Slovak ladies round the fire 'bout getting work on one of these here farms. She's glaring over at her pa when I tell him that I did have a word with 'em, but they said there weren't no work to be got this late in the year.

"Damn liars," Mr. Paul smiles to me. "Them women are damn liars."

He tells me that it's maybe true there ain't much work left, but there sure is some. He pokes Pauline in her ribs a little.

He says to her, "Ain't that right, Paul?" Pauline gives her pa a look that's even meaner than her usual before she admits that, ya, maybe some farmers is still hiring.

"Pauline and me been workin out Lasky's in Reel's Corner for goin on two weeks now," Mr. Paul tells us.

"That right?" my ma asks. Her face lights up at the chance of us getting hired on somewhere.

Mr. Paul says they been picking potatoes out there and shucking cow corn too. He says that five miles is a far piece to go every day, but walking beats starving, so they'll keep on going.

My ma's got them cabbage leafs all cleaned up and she drops them into a pot of cold water with a couple of our cut up potatoes. She tells Frankie to haul the pot over to the cook fire. Esther's got to go with him to make sure he keeps his eye on that pot, cause my ma don't want none of them Tent City Slovaks walking off with any of her pots.

The next morning we're all up before it's even light so we can get something into our stomachs before we hike on up to Lasky's. My ma griddles up some kind of pancakes outta water and that acorn paste. Chewing them turpentine tasting platters apart me and Lottie learn it's hard work to make out like they taste okay. When Mr. Paul and Pauline come by to get us, my ma offers them some poison pancakes, but they says that they had biscuits and ain't hungry no more. Lottie and me sneak them the high sign behind my ma's back while Esther just pretends to put her finger down her throat.

Frankie wants to come long to Lasky's with us, but Mr. Paul figures Lottie and me will have a better chance of getting on if there's just the two of us to hire. So both the twins stay with my ma and Johnny at the tent camp. I tell Frankie to help fetch up water and fire wood and keep his eye on Johnny, make sure none of them tent camp kids try to trick him out outta his shoes. My ma says she's gonna try to get some kind of acorn paste bread baked up for tonight. That gets the lot of us all moving outta the tent camp and hiking up Patchtown Road at a pretty good clip.

Since what happened to Buzzy, the curfew's lightened up so much that the only Pinkerton we see round 40 is sprawled inside a sedan at the Scalp Pike crossroads at the top of 40 Hill. He got his feet leveled up on the dashboard. I don't look too long, but from what I can see, he's more concerned with reading the Johnstown newspaper than keeping his eyes peeled for union men.

Mr. Paul keeps us hiking right quick down into Windber, past Delaney Ball Field and onto the road to Reel's Corner. Pauline and Lottie walk a little behind us peeking in the dress shop windows, jawing 'bout what's nice and what ain't. It's funny to me cause I don't see much chance of either of them getting no store-bought dress any time soon, but I guess not admitting things to yourself is one more way to keep going when skies run dark. Mr. Paul seems a pretty quiet fella in the morning and he don't say much to me, 'cept that I should act real respectful towards Farmer Lasky.

"He's an alright fella then?" I says.

"He's a bastard pure and simple," Mr. Paul tells me. "But showin 'em that respect can make it easier to get along with all kinds a bastards."

We keep going down the road to Reel's Corner, past corn fiels broke up by stretches of pine and stands oak and maple. I'm watching the sky lighten up from blue-red to orange. Maybe it's just cause it's early, but once we get past Windber we don't see even one Cossack. I'm feeling pretty good. It's on my mind what Mr. Paul said 'bout old Lasky though, cause Buzzy would a for sure said about him being a bastard and all, but he never would a thought to do anything other than call him a low down bastard to his face and maybe give him what for if he could and let that be the end of it.

It's full light by the time we hit the dirty turnoff for Lasky's farm. Mr. Paul's right. They're still taking on folks for work. I follow him up onto the side porch of the farmhouse where one of the Lasky boys is finishing off his breakfast. He says most of the other miners has already been set to work in the orchard, so me and Mr. Paul can cool our heels on the back of his horse wagon. He's gonna finish his bacon and then we're gonna make the collection run across the potato fields. Me and Mr. Paul is to take turns walking behind the wagon stacking all the full sacks of potatoes from their fields into the wagon bed. He cracks for Pauline to show Lottie to the barn behind the house and get her started helping out with shucking the cow corn.

Lasky's land runs the whole way from Reel's Corner down to the edge of Old Ashtola, so it ain't no small job getting their potatoes brung in. First turn, Mr. Paul walks behind the wagon and heaves them potato sacks up to me so I can stack them in the back of the wagon while the Lasky boy drives from one field to the next. We see a good many folks working in the fields digging up them potatoes. They carry twenty-pound flour sacks with them, popping the potatoes in a couple at a time. Then they take their sacks over to where they got a pile of fifty-pound bags and folks dump their sacks into them bags.

It's right before we stop to take the lunch break that I see some of them Tent City Slovak women what told me there weren't no work to be got. They're bent over picking potatoes outta the ground on the North Slope above the Ashtola line. I look down at them from the bed of the wagon and I'm thinking that I oughtta say something to them 'bout how they lied to me or maybe how they're stooped over grabbing up them potatoes in the damp. But Mr. Paul sees 'em too and he shakes his head, warning me not to say nothing.

When we finish up with getting the potatoes collected up there, the Lasky boy drives the horse wagon back to the barn so we can get unloaded before we eat our lunch. He buzzes on into the farmhouse to eat with the rest of the Laskys, leaving me and Mr. Paul to unload all of them potato sacks ourselfs before we can hoof it over to the lunch table they got set up on the other side of the barn for the day workers.

When Mr. Paul jumps outta the wagon. I slide the fifty-pound sacks across the wagon bed and toss them down to him and he piles them in the wheelbarrow. Then he hauls them cross the barn, and we stack them up so Mr. Lasky can drive 'em into Windber mid-winter when the prices go up.

I'm glad Mr. Paul's a big fella, cause if I had to take my fair share of turns catching them sacks, I'd be too tired to eat before we even got anywhere near to finished. I wait till we're stacking up the last of the potato sacks before I ask Mr. Paul about how come he didn't want me saying nothing to them Slovak women. I say that he knows as well as me that they tried to trick me into not looking for no work.

Mr. Paul bites off a little piece from a plug of tobacco. Then he puts his head out the barn door to make sure that no one's walking round out there before he sets down on the back of the horse wagon. He holds the tobacco plug out to me and I grab it and shred a bite off with my teeth.

"Them women out in those fields ain't got nobody to look out for 'em, Chester," Mr. Paul says. "So, they're doin the best they can to look out for themselfs."

"We all gotta look out for ourselfs," I says.

Mr. Paul nods and spits out some tobacco juice onto the floor of Lasky's barn. He says that I should think about what it'd be like for my ma, if she didn't have Lottie and me and she was trying to raise up Johnny and the twins on her own. Running the cloth of one of them empty potato sacks between my fingers, I set there thinking about how hard it was for my ma to pull herself up off the neighbor's porch the day the Cossack give us the boot out.

Before he jumps down off the wagon, Mr. Paul also reminds me that I just got here and starting up trouble ain't gonna say much for keeping me on.

He don't wait for me to answer back to that. He just says he's hungry as hell and we oughtta get on over to the lunch table before them damn Slovak women eat up every last thing. I follow him outside, round the barn to the back of Lasky's house.

Them Laskys got maybe fifteen miners and their wifes from all the tent camps round Windber set down at a long wood slab table behind their house. I see Lottie over on the corner setting next to Pauline drinking cups of coffee. Everybody looks like they're pretty much done eating and there ain't nothing left on the table 'cept a little mashed potatoes and a couple of thin beans. It ain't much, but it's still a damn sight better than any kind of acorn anything, so I grab what I can.

I set myself down across from Lottie and say hey to her and just nod and try to steer clear of Pauline. Lottie says that we should have got here quicker cause there was a whole mess of vegetables and fried chicken too.

I try to listen when Mr. Paul talks to the other men down the table about what he thinks is gonna happen with the strike, but a whole bunch of fellas all come stomping up from stacking apple crates in the orchard barn across the road. They're mostly miners from down 35, but I recognize Fatty Papinchak from 40 and Goose Naylor too, who I ain't seen since he got Blacklisted for buying mining tools on discount somewhere out around Saint Michael instead of paying for 'em high dollar at the Eureka Company Store—and sunafabitch if

Grubby Koshinsky, that big mouth from the union meeting, ain't there with 'em. They're all loud and hungry and pushing their way up to the table. Grubby's running his mouth as usual, saying for anybody what already ate to get the hell up and get back to work so they can set.

Lottie and Pauline and most of the other folks what was shucking cow corn pop up to get back to it, but there still ain't enough seats for everybody. Fatty, who used to be a track layer down 35, tries to take my seat off of me, but I tell him that I just got here and he better plan on putting that big butt of his somewhere else. At first I think he's gonna start a fuss, but then one of the Lasky women comes off the porch toting a fresh plate of steaming chicken and Fatty would just as soon miss the Resurrection of the Body as a crack at one of them chicken legs.

All the men at the table grab up that chicken fast as they can. When I reach out to get a piece for myself, Grubby takes hold of my arm. He says to me that I already ate and this here chicken is for the orchard workers.

"I ain't had none yet," I says to him.

But he don't let go of my arm till I stick my fork into his wrist a little and then he stands up and starts making a big enough fuss that all the men at the table turn to eye up the two of us. Grubby says to everybody that he's trying to stop me from getting extra chicken. I'm looking to Mr. Paul to give him hell, but he don't stand or even raise up his voice, just whispers for Grubby to set back the hell down.

"One a them Laskys come out here and sacks us cause a your fooling round Grubby, there ain't gonna be nothing to stop me from beating the Everloving Christ right outta you," Mr. Paul says soft, but nobody doubts he means it. "Now let that boy have a damn piece a chicken."

So I get my chicken, but before I even get it into my mouth I hear Grubby start kicking. He's telling Goose that just cause Mr. Paul used to be fire boss down 35, he still thinks he can tell everybody what to do. It's funny, cause instead of saying anything back to Grubby, Goose Naylor starts talking loud to me.

"Hey Chester," he says. "Ya ever hear how Grubby got his name?"

Goose don't gimme no chance to answer before he says even louder to the whole damn table that when Grubby was little, his name used to be Frank. But he was such a pig at every mealtime that his own father started on calling him Grubby, cause he was out to get all the grub for himself and not leave none for nobody else.

Goose says, "Hell, Grubby likes food so much, he even keeps a little something extra in his straggly beard. Just in case he gets hungry after lunch."

Everybody laughs pretty good at this 'cept Grubby, who's looking daggers at me and Goose both. Even Fatty, who ain't partial to food jokes, rubs his big belly and gives a snort and we start back into our lunch. But by then, them Laskys is done with their own eating and they have me and Mr. Paul get back to the fields and all the other fellas gotta get a move on back over to the orchard.

Later in the afternoon I get took off of potato collecting and put into the barn with Lottie and Pauline and a bunch of old folks to shuck cow corn. They also stick Grubby in there to do the wheelbarrowing, so maybe he made friends as good in the orchard as he done at the lunch table.

Them Laskys got a bunch of us setting round in the circle on top of old crates. We strip the cow corn down to the ear while Grubby hauls what's shucked over to the other end of the barn to the hen house, so they can put it up as feed for the chickens in the deep winter.

Pulling them brown husks off that corn ain't much fun, I'll tell you, but it beats the hell outta trying to catch fifty-pound potato sacks getting tossed off the back of a wagon. Setting there between Lottie and Pauline, a big stack of corn husks in front of me, I see that every time Grubby wheels a load of corn in from the other side of the barn, he gives me the evil eye. I don't know what he thinks he's gonna pull in front of all these people, but I'm keeping my eye on him.

After working them corn ears for most of the afternoon, we get a little break at the table outside. They give us maybe fifteen minutes to have some coffee and cornbread and catch our breath. Then they herd us back into the barn to get settled down again to stripping them husks.

None of them old shuckers talk too much while they're working, but some of the *studda babas* sing songs in Slovak or Hungarian. Since they're all about the Blessed Virgin and stuff like that, I don't really listen much.

Mostly, I'm thinking 'bout what Mr. Paul said about causing trouble not saying much for keeping me on. Like with Grubby at lunch, I wanna make sure to get treated fair, but I don't want to go get myself fired off of here. Maybe Grubby's thinking the same thing cause he didn't even come out with us for the break. Ever since we come back into the barn he quit paying me any mind. He just shovels up them stripped corn ears and dumps them in the bin next to the chicken coop like anybody else. Then he goes back to the other side of the barn for another load.

I keep on at shucking them small ears of hard corn and it's somewhere in the middle of my third or fourth bushel after the break that I pull the husks off a red ear. All of them old timers are looking at me and they're laughing to beat the band. They're all saying, "Now, we'll see who he likes!"

I don't understand what's going on till Lottie explains it to me. She tells me that when any man who ain't got no wife shucks off a red ear of corn, he can kiss any woman that ain't got no husband.

"It ain't that he can," one of them Slovak women says to her. "It's that he *has* to."

"Has to?" I ask her.

"Has to!"

All of them shuckers agree. Even the one Lasky boy they got keeping an eye on us says so. I gotta pick one of the girls to kiss. And that girl's gotta let me. So, I'm looking round that barn and my choices are making me a little nervous. If I ask to kiss my own sister, it's gonna look awful strange, and none of them old Slovak women are looking so good. So, this pretty much leaves me with trying to kiss Pauline, who's fine as a girl can get, but she looks like she'd rather load six tons of pea coal for free than have my lips pushed up next to hers.

Them old folks is yelling for me to pick somebody. They're teasing me pretty good, asking me what I'm waiting for. Pauline turns towards me and her smooth skin is white as cow's milk and her lips are awful full and it looks to me like there's maybe just the littlest bit of softness sneaking into her blue eyes. She bends over so her mouth is pretty close to my ear. I twist towards her so I can hear what she's gonna whisper to me.

She says, "Just get it over with trapper boy."

I gives Pauline a quick peck on the cheek and hope that will put the whole thing to rest, but all the people in the barn are hooting and jeering, saying, "Whatta hell!" and "What kinda kiss izzat?" and such. Folks are teasing Pauline even more than me, calling her Prude-line and stuff like that.

This must make Pauline awful mad, cause she reaches out and grabs hold of the back of my head by the hair and pulls my face right into hers, pressing her lips hard to mine. I don't even get no chance to think about it, the whole thing happens so fast. All I know is that I want it to happen again.

When Pauline pulls her face back away, she looks plain flat beautiful with that long blonde hair reaching down to her shoulders and eyes blue and bright as the summer sky after coming outta 40 mine on a double shift. The people around us are cheering and laughing. Some are clapping and one of them old Slovak men says, "Now there's a girl with spirit."

But this don't last long neither, because old Farmer Lasky comes running into the barn. He got that damn Grubby Koshinsky with him and they're both hollering blue murder 'bout something. That's when I notice Grubby is pointing his finger straight at me and there's only one word coming outta his mouth, "Thief!"

FOURTEEN

So, I guess Grubby had a good reason to be smiling instead of giving me the evil eye after we finished up the afternoon break. The sunafabitch swiped a half-dozen eggs outta Lasky's hen house and snuck every one of them into the waist pockets of my Peacoat when I left it setting in the barn to have that coffee. Then he slid off and told Farmer Lasky that he seen me creeping into the hen house when folks was sitting at the table eating their corn bread.

Damn Lasky chased me and Lottie outta that barn so quick, half the people there probably thought it was for kissing Pauline. We had to hoof it the whole way back to Tent City without even getting no potatoes or nothing for stacking potatoes and stripping corn ears the whole blessed day.

My ma sure ain't jumping for joy when she sees me and Lottie come strolling up through the scrub woods before dark empty handed. I spin her out the whole story while she twists herself up on the flat of a moss carpeted rock in front of our tent. Darning Esther's Sunday dress with flour sack pieces she bleached out down Paint Creek, she's sewing faster and faster listening to what happened. By the end, she's cursing Grubby and cursing damn Lasky too.

But my ma is serious as a snapping brace when she says she don't know what we're gonna do come next week, cause all the money we got in the world is the three dollars she got when she sold our furniture to the Slovaks. Lottie smiles with her lips squished together and says we'll think of something. Then she snatches up one of them acorn buckets and heads off into the woods.

I take account of what we got left foodwise. My ma's right—maybe five, six days at most. I plop down onto a seat over by the cook fire trying to stay warm and waiting for Mr. Paul to come back from Lasky's and see what he's got to say 'bout this whole mess.

Watching the dark smoke curdling out of the fire pit, I huddle myself there till it's full dark. Missing Buzzy so much it's hard to look at anything without it reminding me of him, I mostly keep my eyes squinted into the pit. I stare at them thick logs catching fire in the heat coming off the coal and think about how some things in this world ain't got no choice, they just gotta turn into whatever's closest to them. I can see now how come Buzzy was so worked up about the curfew coming down. That liquor money wasn't just keeping us fed, it was the only thing keeping us in the house. How was he gonna head up a family that's tented out in the scrub woods like a pack of gypsies?

When Mr. Paul does come, he don't look none too happy neither. He says Lasky damn near fired him and Pauline both off the farm just for recommending me.

It surprises me some, but Pauline is taking my side. She's wagging her finger at her pa, arguing that I couldn't have stole them eggs cause I was setting next to her for the whole break. She's flat out sure, cause it was damn near making her stomach turn to watch the way I was pushing my corn bread down to bring up the dregs of my coffee cup.

"I really don't know what to tell ya, Chester," Mr. Paul says to me.

He says that he believes me and all 'bout not stealing them eggs, but it don't matter much one way or the other. Even if there was other farms looking for hands, between me being labeled a thief and my brother being shot down as a murderer, I got as good a chance of being named Burgess of Windber as I do getting hired on by any of them farmers.

While we're talking, my ma comes round dishing up slices of that black acorn bread and plattering out some of the corn and beans that Mr. Paul brung from Lasky's. It's starting to get colder and there's a bit of rain drizzle coming down, so most of the Tent City families is either setting in their tents or huddled up under the big tarp next to the cook fire.

There's maybe twenty of us clustered there and we're lucky cause a Hungarian fella tossed a bucket of pea coal into the wood fire before he called it quits for the night, so there's a pretty good blaze reaching up outta the fire pit. I'm setting next to Lottie and watching Mr. Paul talking to Pauline at the other side of the fire. That Pauline really looks like something in that fire light. I'm thinking about her lips and the way she stuck up for me about getting fired off of Lasky's. Even the way her hair catches that light flickering is like to get me six different kinds of distracted.

"Ya know she likes ya, Chet," Lottie says to me.

"Who?"

"Don't ya ask me who!" Lottie laughs.

Then Lottie pops up away from the fire saying she's going to help ma with Esther's dress. I keep setting there trying to figure out what I'm gonna do. Another week of living in this tent camp with nothing coming into the kitty, we'll be broker than a Chinaman's clock.

Setting there with my ass flat on that cold rock, watching the fire die down I'm thinking 'bout what Buzzy would do to get us ahead if he was here. But I can't go hitting nobody over the head with a rail spike and taking their wallet. And it ain't just a matter of morals. Buzzy was a hell of a lot bigger than me.

Then I realize that ain't what Buzzy would a done at all. At least it ain't what he *did* do. I'm picturing Buzzy jawing with Facianni down the 40 Hotel about the curfew and that twitch-lipped Coulson clueing me in on how we kept our house for so long during the strike. When the chips was down, Buzzy saw clear how to keep us outta the tent camps—hauling liquor for the Black Hand.

I stare again across the fire at Pauline and her pa. She's looking real fine to me, but I know that if my family's gonna get outta this camp with our asses intact, she ain't the one that I gotta go have a word with.

FIFTEEN

Next morning, my ma gives me a dime outta what money we got left, and I hoof it up over the bony piles, edge the Slovak cemetery and head back down into the West End of Windber to Dago Town, where I ain't been anywhere near since that night with Buzzy. I almost feel like I'm on the look out for ghosts when I pass by them wops' markets and bakeries. The sun's in the middle of a blue sky and it's warm as September, but I keep both my hands buried down deep in my britches pockets, fingering that silver and thinking 'bout just how I'm gonna try to talk Facianni into giving me a job.

When I pass Leone's Market on Twelve Street and come up on Facianni's barbershop, my legs want to just keep hiking, maybe take the dime and head on up to Kinjelko's and buy some stew beef, then hoof it quick and quiet back to 40 to cook up some dinner, but I figure with the spot we're in, I ain't got no choice. I slow to a shuffle and try to catch a gander inside of the shop before I pull open Facianni's door.

First off, I spot the fella what come chasing after us to warn Buzzy about the Pinkertons the night they got him. Both him and the other Eye-tie what was with him when Facianni come down to see Buzzy at the 40 Hotel are setting in two red leather chairs at the window. Facianni's got some baldheaded, flabby wop plopped down in his barber chair, setting for a shave, but when I yank open the door to his place, he looks up from that dago's neck long enough to give me a good once over.

I stroll past his big dagos, fat and thin, without looking at them and set myself down in the next leather chair, closest to the razor strap. Easing my *dupa* down into that highback chair, I watch Facianni draw that straight razor cross the face of that heavy set dago. He's real quick with the shimmering blade and don't miss a beat stripping the lather off of them big old jowls.

When the bald dago gets up, he digs a few nickels outta his britches and trickles them into Facianni's hand. Facianni keeps his mitt right where it is. He stares at that dago like he oughtta know better, till the fella reaches his hand deep into his hip pocket and busts out a greenback.

"Next!" Facianni says.

He stands there clutching the handle of that straight razor while the lumpy wop slips his arms into his coatsleeves and makes for the door. I watch little white dollops of shaving foam slide off the business edge of Facianni's silver and plop down onto the linoleum. The fatter of the two chair setting wops says something about if a fella's gonna play them numbers he better be ready to pony it when they don't come up.

Facianni got a round face and small dark hands and his thin, black hair is all slicked back onto the flat of his head with some kind of barber oil. He ain't wearing no necktie, but he's got a white collar fixed to his shirt. When I get up standing right next to him, I can see he ain't but an inch or two taller than me.

After I lower myself down into the barber chair, he gives it a few pumps with his foot, raising me up and says to me that I'm looking too young to shave, so I must have come in wanting a haircut.

"Just a little off the sides," I tell him. I'm hoping this might cost less than a full hair cutting.

Facianni says he ain't never seen me in his shop before.

"That's true," I tell him. "Most pollocks don't come down this way for a haircut."

"Most pollocks ain't got no money for a haircut," one of them big fellas laughs.

I don't pay no mind, but I tell Facianni that he seen me before.

"You got a look at me in the 40 Hotel," I says, "when ya come down to talk to my brother about the big curfew coming down."

Facianni pulls a big white bib off a hook on the wall and snugs it round my neck. He snatches up a big ol pair of silver barber shears off the counter, sets my head straight with his fingers and starts clipping away at the blond hair round my ears.

"Buzzy was yer brother?" he asks me.

"That's right," I says, "I'm Chester Pistakowski."

"Wuzza damn shame what happened ta him," he says. "Wuzza good boy, Buzzy. Good man."

Facianni keeps on with them shears, trimming up the back of my hair, snipping a little off the top. I watch his face in the big square mirror in front of the barber chair. His thumb twists my ear sideways and the sharp tip of them scissors scrapes at against the skin behind. Cutting slow, he bends down so close I can smell the old man breath stinking outta his mouth. I hear them metal scissor blades scraping quick together while he clips one side of my head, then the other.

My mouth's getting dry and I can feel my heart speeding up and my back dampening the leather back of his barber chair. I think to myself this is what ya come for Chester. Don't make no hash of it now.

"My brother used to do a little work for ya," I says to Facianni.

Facianni don't say nothing to this, just turns my head to the side and keeps them scissors snapping away at pretty good clip as his moves along to the front of my head.

"Course he never told me nothin 'bout what he done," I tell him.

"Buzzy could keep his mouth shut." Facianni nods to me. "Maybe that runs in the family?"

"I ain't sayin."

Facianni smiles and steps away from the barber chair over towards the counter. He grabs a round silver mirror. He moves the mirror around behind my head showing off to me different angles of where my hair meets the back of my neck.

"Whatcha think, Chester Pistakowski?"

"I think maybe you might have some kinda job for me," I says. "I mean with the big curfew done with and all."

One of them big dagos setting by the door starts up laughing, saying that I got pretty big balls coming in here and talking like this.

"Angelo Facianni don't offer no jobs to just any pollock what comes stumbling in off the street.," he laughs.

But Facianni, he ain't laughing one bit. He's just looking at my reflection in the mirror—like he's doing some kind of math in his head and I'm one of the numbers.

"Ya drive a horse wagon alright, Chester?" he asks me.

I tell him that I'm a real good driver. Facianni nods and takes them scissors over to the razor strap. He runs them up and down that strap fast and slick, smooth. Bringing them up to his eye to look them over, he tells me he just might have some kinda job for me. I better come back tonight after dark and give a holler round the backdoor of his shop.

It's like I'm right on top of the world marching outta that barbershop into the sunshine, but I try not to let any of them chair-sitting dagos see nothing of what's in my head at all. It ain't till I round the corner outta Dago Town and get back to Swede Street that I even let a smile come cross my face.

When I get back to the Tent City, I still got that grin going strong. Lottie and my ma are huddled up on the log outside our tent finishing Esther's dress. Lottie gets a peek at me smiling and starts hassling me 'bout how come I look so damn happy.

"Must be all this good weather," I says.

But Lottie ain't nowhere near ready to take that for an answer and keeps right after me. When I see our ma ain't looking, I give a quick point for Lottie to meet me inside our tent to give her the scoop on where I been. When she gets inside the tent, I shut down the flaps. It's half dark and the air is close. She laughs and says to me that I don't gotta hide nothing, cause Pauline ain't even around. I tell her that this ain't got nothing to do with Pauline.

"Oh, I seen the way you was lookin at her when she was settin by the fire last night, Chester," she says. "There's some things a woman just knows."

Lottie turns away from me to start laying out the pillows, blankets and the feather ticks we got left for tonight. She says to me that I don't gotta worry none anyway, cause Pauline likes me too.

"She likes ya just fine ever since her pa tolt her 'bout how ya stood up for Charlie Dugan at the union meetin."

"What?"

"Mr. Paul told Pauline how ya give it to Grubby and all the rest of them Fair Weatherers when they wanted to quit on the strike. Now that Pauline knows ya ain't nothin like Buzzy, she's real keen for ya. She said she didn't even mind kissin ya in Lasky's barn."

Now that Pauline knows I ain't like Buzzy, she's real keen on me. Don't that just beat all, I'm thinking to myself. The one day in my whole damn life that I really am like Buzzy and sunafabitch if it ain't today.

"Pauline says she might have even kissed ya again if that liar Grubby hadn't a got ya fired off Lasky's."

"I don't know what to tell ya," I says to Lottie. "I think you're makin the whole thing up."

I pick up one of Lottie's feather pillows and slap it so hard into the side of the tent, one of the canvas walls collapses before I go stomping outta there spitting and kicking rocks outta my path the whole way to Patchtown Road.

Sixteen

When the sun's near down, I roust my *dupa* off the stump I been loafing on in the 35 woods and follow the Penn Central tracks down through Dago Town back to Facianni's barber shop. I keep myself out of sight hiding in the shadow of the freight cars, waiting for full dark. When a horse wagon comes rolling up the alley to the side of the West End company store, I push forward between the wheels of the coal cars so I can get a peek at who's driving. Up on the buckboard, slouched back into the seat, the thinner dago what was bitching about us pollocks not having no money is clutching the reins. His shoulders is hunched up around his neck which is long like a stovepipe. His adam's apple's so big I can see it bobbing when he starts to mumbling up one of them dago songs.

I wait till he stops the wagon at the back door of the shop before I slip out from the coal cars and make my way down the alley. Keeping my back pressed tight against the wall of the company store, I watch him knock a couple times on the back door of the barber shop. The varnished door edges open and somebody skids out two waist high stacks of wooden liquor cases. The dago sneaks a look down the other end of the alley towards the Windber station and then snatches up one of the cases and hefts it into the back of the wagon.

"Lemme give ya a hand," I says to him.

That dago damn near jumps outta his skin when he hears my voice coming out from the other side of that horse wagon. He lets the case clatter down onto the wood bed of the wagon. I don't hear no glass breaking, but he's for sure one pissed off dago, saying to me that any broken bottles are coming outta my pay.

"So you break 'em and I pay for 'em?" I says. "Don't sound right to me."

I know I'm being a real smart ass here, but it feels like with these fellas ya gotta stand up for yourself right off the bat. When the door of the barber shop opens up Facianni sticks his head out just far enough that I can see his hat brim.

"Shutta hell up, you two," he says.

In the back of the barber shop there are three more cases of liquor stacked up by the door. Facianni tells me the dago's name is Sal and we're supposed to take all of this liquor out to Dunlo.

"Ya take to Sons a Itlee," he says. "Ya get ten dollars."

I start to say that sounds good to me, but Facianni's already walking back towards the front of the shop. I grab up a case of liquor, and Sal heaves up the other two and we take 'em out to the wagon. Sal pushes the back door shut, real careful not to make no noise and then we stretch a piece of canvas over top of the liquor crates in the back end of the wagon.

When we climb up in the wagon seat, I set myself down to ride shotgun, but Sal shoves the reins into my hands. He says that everybody knows he can do this job, it's me that's got something to prove here. So, I take up the reins and drive the wagon nice and slow up Railroad Alley onto Somerset Avenue past Leone's Market to the corner of Ninth Street.

"Getta move on, ya dumb pollock," Sal says to me. "Ya don't wanna make it look like yer doin something wrong."

So, I give them reins a shake and the horses giddup a bit and we're headed up past the Berwinds' Big Office to get onto 160 outta town. I'm stewing over that dumb pollock shit a little, but I figure if I'm gonna be working with all these damn dagos, I better just learn to let it roll off my back.

Once we make the turn onto Dunlo Road and start rolling up the big hill, it's all kraut farmers' cornfields and I figure we're pretty much in the clear. I look round a bit at the bare trees, thinking that I'm doing all right for myself. Just last night I was setting round, fired off of Lasky's and worried about starving. And now here I am, gonna earn ten dollars in one night.

Setting next to me, Sal ain't saying nothing. He's just whistling some song I don't know and sluggin off a bottle of wine. I flip my coat collar up so's it covers my neck and I snap the reins again. The less time this whole trip takes, the better.

We're going along pretty good, already past Windber Recreation Park where they got the Fourth of July picnic, when I spot a wagon up ahead. It ain't moving towards us or away from us. It's just setting there on the side of the road.

"Sal," I says. "What ya make a that?"

"Maybe they got a busted wheel, kid. How the hell do I know?"

Sal tries not to let nothing get into his voice, but I can tell he ain't too happy 'bout seeing this wagon. I watch him reach his hand into his coat pocket. He fidgets out a little black revolver. He looks clumsy with it, like he ain't used to fooling with no pistol. It's scuffed and small in his hand, nicked up fierce, and nothing like them chrome shining forty-fives that ride on the Pinkertons' hip. But when Sal clicks the dark hammer back, it dawns on me. This is some serious business.

"Keep drivin," Sal says.

The closer we get to that wagon, the quicker my breath is coming. If this turns into some kinda shootout, I ain't even got no gun and Sal don't look like no Buffalo Bill to me. What if there's a whole mess of them and only two of us? I try to listen for anything they're saying but I can't hear nothing over top of our wheels clacking on the road.

"Aw, for Chrissake!" Sal says.

For a second, I think he's mad at me for slowing the wagon down, but then I see he's squinting ahead at the folks up off the side of the road. Sal wipes his nose with the back of his hand and then eases the pistol hammer back down before he cuddles it back into his pocket.

"Damn Windber cops," he laughs. "For a second, I thought you and me was in some deep trouble."

When we pull up alongside the police wagon, there's two Windber police setting on the buckboard. They got navy uniforms like the Pinkertons but with copper badges instead of brass buttons and brimmed captain's hats instead of slouch caps. Sal talks to them real quiet for a minute, till they're all smiling and joking.

"This here's Chester." Sal points at me with his thumb. "He's working for "some people" now."

After them cops take a good look at my mug, Sal gives 'em a twenty-dollar bill outta his hip pocket. The cops chuckle a little more and give me a nod and say "thanks" to Sal.

The police closest to our wagon pops off his captain's hat and tucks the greenback inside the silk lining. Then his partner snaps the reins a good one and turns the wagon back around cross the road and they head off for Windber. Sal watches them till they're pretty far gone down the road into the dark.

"Angelo's got every one a them Windber cops in his back pocket," he says to me. "A twenty-dollar bill can get you loose of most anything you're gonna pull."

"That's good to know," I says.

"But I tell ya, kid," Sal smiles, all cock of the walk. "Don't try none a that shit with them State Police. You'll get pinched for liquor and bribing to boot."

I nod at this, but it don't matter none, cause Sal ain't lookin. He got the reins clutched in his hands now and he ain't in no mood to go slow. He's slapping them horses into a lather and we're making time hauling ass down Dunlo Road. The wind zips over my skin with a chill and them trees are just shadows dropping away behind us. Ain't even no use in trying to talk over the clatter of them horse wagon wheels on the reddog.

We keep going like that for almost a whole hour before we get to Main Street in Dunlo. I'm rubbing my hands together trying to keep 'em from freezing straight off till Sal tosses me back the reins. He takes a heavy pull from his wine bottle and says driving this damn wagon is thirsty work. Smiling at me, he says he wants to get his ass back to Windber cause there's a card game going out in 42 and his good luck feels fixed as a fat lady's wedding ring.

He points for me to make the turn on Fifth Street behind a two-story brick Sons of Italy Club. I stop short of the back door and Sal hops outta the wagon. He tells me to stay put and goes over and gives the same knock I seen him use at Facianni's. When the door opens up, three fellas come shuffling out. They're all in dungarees and Sal looks pretty fancy next to them in his serge trousers and buttondown shirt.

"This here is Buzzy's brother." Sal jerks his thumb up at me in the wagon seat. "He's going to be drivin for Angelo now."

Them rough looking fellas just nod their heads at Sal and start counting out his money.

SEVENTEEN

Six weeks of hauling that bootleg liquor for Angelo and my whole life is different. I turned fifteen. I got my family moved clean outta Tent City and set up down Dago Town. I'm getting 'em the star boarder treatment living above Leone's Market. We got storebought furniture and beds and we're eating halushki and blintzes every day. We even had ham shank and gold crust cherry pie steaming on the table at Christmas. The twins are back in the oneroom and even Lottie, who ain't none too happy 'bout me turned to bootlegging, seems have a little spring back her step. My ma's maybe a little worried 'bout me, but since she knows that we was damn well gonna starve staying in that tent camp, she ain't gonna kick neither.

Only thing bothering me, I ain't seen Mr. Paul or Pauline neither for a good while now. I been too busy with this here bootlegging to be scuttling around down that tent camp or freezing out on the picket line. 'Sides, Lottie's done told me five times a day that Pauline would rather marry a monkey than be caught dead running round with low life bootleggers.

Down at the 40 Hotel barroom, I heard tale from Fatty Papinchak that Charlie Dugan and them might be having some kind of luck with the Berwinds over Philadelphia. They been talking to a posse of newspaper reporters 'bout coming down to Windber and writing how old Berwind's getting rich selling top dollar coal to the subway trains while he's doing us dirt. I don't know nothing exactly, cause I been busting my ass day and night for Angelo.

So far, I been to Dunlo and Vintondale and Seanor and Hollsopple and Hyndman and damn near every other town on the Route 160 and 56 T. I been to so many "Sons a Itlee" I'm getting to feel like I'm some kinda wop my own self. I even got a new set of clothes for myself so when them small town dagos see me comin they know right off that I'm working for Angelo.

Tonight, I'm headed over to his standalone down on 18th Street. Me and Sal gotta water down the bathtub liquor Angelo gets from the Ashtola moonshiners before we pour it into Gordon's gin bottles. Then I gotta run the lot of 'em to the Slovak Club out in Beaverdale.

When I get down to that cellar, Sal's already got most of the bottles full of bootleg and he tells me to get to work behind him, topping off all them fifths with a bit of real Gordon's to keep them Beaverdale Slovaks from getting wise.

We're going at it in one of the extra rooms that Angelo had dug out under his front yard to the side of his coal bin. He keeps all the liquor down here, the Canadian stuff that comes in from Pittsburgh and the bootleg too. Ain't too many fellas, outside of the Black Handers theirselves, that know just what he keeps down here. I'm pretty sure Angelo didn't even tell Buzzy where the mix up was being handled.

"Ya wanna learn something, kid?" Sal asks me.

I step over to the plywood table that Sal's working on. He's dousing a mix of water and moonshine outta a gallon vinegar jug into a row of washed out Gordon's bottles. He clues me in that if I spread each gallon of bathtub over twelve bottles instead of eight, I can make up a whole extra case that I can sell for myself.

I tell Sal that's pretty good thinking. But I ain't looking to get into no trouble with Angelo, so I mix my bottles the way I been told. When everything's ready, I straw pack all the bottles into apple crates and carry 'em up the stairs and stack them up in Angelo's wagon.

The ride out to Beaverdale is all right. Nothing but moonlight and white stars and the wind whistling through the bone bare trees. I'm singing a little song about pork chops and thick legged women Buzzy taught me while we was loading egg coal on the B seam last winter. I wonder if maybe he sung the same song on the same run.

Them Slovaks, I think, are pretty happy to be getting any liquor at all, so they're all backslaps and smiles with teeth. They pay me cash money and then haul the whole stack of liquor crates into the Slovak Hall theirselfs, so I don't even have to get down from the seat of the wagon.

It's coming back that I hit a snag. I'm clipping along the 160 down into Windber when I see a dark sedan setting over next to the park entrance. I don't pay it no mind thinking that maybe it's broke down or something. But once I get past, it fires up and stays on my tail around the bend and down the hill, creeping after me the whole way to where I hang my left onto Somerset Avenue.

Sick of being followed, I draw the wagon over on the corner of Tenth Street in front of the dago baker. I figure that sedan's gonna pass me by and keep going straight into Windber, but the bastard drifts in behind me. I start getting nervous, twisting my head around, trying to catch a peek at who's walking up on me. Angelo says ain't no other dagos gonna give me a hassle long as I work for him. He says even them rough Sicilians ain't gonna bother with me neither, cause they keep to themselves down Johnstown and he takes care of Windber, but I don't know.

It ain't none of them wild dagos, though. It's that twitch-faced Coulson, 'cept now he's gotta wide-brim Trooper hat balanced on his head like he's some kind of State Police.

He comes strutting up the side of the wagon and that's when I see he got the star pinned to the side of his greatcoat.

"What ya got in the back a that wagon, boy?" he asks me.

"Coulson," I says. "I ain't got a damn thing in the back of this wagon."

He shines his lantern up all across the buckboard, maybe scanning to make sure I ain't got no shotgun. Then he pushes the light close up into my face and that's when he recognizes me.

"Pistakowski," he asks me. "Why you out so late?"

"Just getting some air," I tell him.

He takes his hat off and puts his other hand on his hip. Hiking one of his high-polish boots up on the wagon wheel, he taps his Trooper's star with his fingertip. He says he knows just what my brother done on the late-night wagon trips. He says he wouldn't be one bit surprised, I ain't up to the same damn thing.

"I bet yer new boss up the State Police barracks would love to learn how ya know so much about hauling Ashtola shine," I tell him.

"I'm gonna check the back of yer wagon."

"I tell ya, I ain't got nothin."

But Coulson's already back there ripping the canvas off the wagon bed. He yanks it down with one quick pull and tosses it into the road. He gives everything back there a toss, but don't find nothing 'cept some straw and an empty apple crate. Spitting some tobacco on the ground, he tells me that I better watch my ass from here on out.

"Cause ya know that I'll be watchin it."

I think 'bout saying he shouldn't spend too much time looking at boys' asses cause "people might talk," but I ain't sure he's a hundred percent above using the blackjack and I ain't looking to get no beating. So, I just let the whole thing go.

Once he rolls off, I hop down and stuff the canvas back into the ass end of the wagon and drive the rest of the way back into Windber humming and thinking about Pauline.

Eighteen

Pushed up close to the dark bar down the 40 Hotel three days later, I'm sipping on a coffee mug of hard cider. I'm dead beat from running a load of corn whiskey the whole way out to Stoystown for some dago's wedding. It's past four o'clock in the afternoon, and the barroom's filled with fellas who are putting in a day here and there, working some of them shoestring mines out toward Central City. But it's getting colder and with most everything used up, folks are having a tough time. The union can't be pitching a fit about every fella that's working for one of them small operators just enough days to keep his family from starving or freezing.

Finishing off my cider, I'm wondering if making the switch to afternoon runs is gonna be enough to throw Coulson off the scent. That's when I spot Little Mikey setting underneath the dartboard across the barroom. He sees me too and comes running over to the bar. He yanks hisself up onto the stool next to me.

"How ya been, Chet?" he says.

I ain't seen Mikey since right after the 40 Station Riot, and I'm still thinking maybe Mikey's the one who let it slip about Buzzy giving it to that dago behind McKluskey's.

"I been up Vintondale," he tells me.

I don't say nothing to him and look straight over the bar and into the mirror at the barroom behind us. Mikey skids his stool over closer to me, like I ain't said nothing cause the barroom is so loud. He's talking all high-pitched and cheerful, like he's real glad to see me. I'm thinking 'bout busting my coffee mug right across his nose. I just set there fuming, listening to him drivel on and on.

"I been helpin my Uncle Val with his farm, Chet," he says. "Them pigs stink to high heaven, but we got the bacon and the sausage near every day."

He stops talking like he's just remembering something. "I'm sorry about Buzzy," he says. "Bout what they done to him."

I wrap my fingers around my mug all careful like, ready to go. I ask Mikey exactly how long he been slopping hogs up Vintondale. He counts on his fingers and tells me he been up there for eight weeks this time.

"Eight weeks, this time," I says. "How 'bout last time?"

"Jesus, Chet. I don't know. I can't remember."

I tell him that he better remember. But he says that he don't have no idea how long. We set at the bar quiet for a minute before I finally turn to look Mikey in his face.

"I need to ask ya somethin, Mikey," I says.

"Anything, Chet," he says to me. "You and me is buddies."

"How come they sent you up Vintondale?"

"I told ya. I went to help my Uncle Val. His kids is grown and he needed some help with all 'em pigs," he says. "Besides, with this strike on and no money comin in, my pa thought one less mouth to feed would help out round here."

"Did ya ever tell anybody 'bout what happened to that dago?"

"Hell no!" he says. "Why would I say anythin 'bout that?"

"Calm down," I says. "Ya sure ya never said nothin?"

I buy Mikey three mugs of hard cider and give him the third degree for a good while. I ask him 'bout how long he was back in 40 before his old man shipped his ass back to mess with them pigs. I grill him good, asking him about who he talked to down Windber and what he said. By the end he's near three sheets, but I'm pretty sure he was only back in 40 for three or four days and the only time his pap let him loose was when he went down to the 40 Hotel for our checker game.

"Ya didn't really think I squealed? Did ya, Chet?"

"Nah," I tell him.

I pull out a tobacco plug, but even inside the barroom, I can't hardly even smell the tobacco in my nose cause of the sulfur stink come blowing off the rock dump. Setting there, working the tobacco into my cheek, I'm thinking if it wasn't Mikey slipping up that put the finger on Buzzy, there must be somebody else what give him up to the damn Pinkertons. It's just a question of finding out who.

Before I can get outta there, Mikey asks me 'bout my new clothes. How come they're so fancy and so clean? I tell him they ain't that fancy and they ain't that clean, he just been spending too much time fooling with them damn pigs.

He laughs and I get my butt up off of the bar stool and say goodnight to Mikey, but before I walk out, I leave a dime setting on the bar for him to get hisself one more mug of that hard cider.

Before I even get the wagon parked out back of Leone's, Frankie comes clattering down the back steps of the rooms we're letting. He's shouting across the alley to me that he'll feed the horse and brush it too if I give him a penny to get some rock candy.

"You'll brush that horse, penny or no penny," I says. "What ya think pays for us to live here?"

"Drivin a horse."

I says 'damn right' driving a horse. Frankie says to me that he wants to drive a horse too someday. I just laugh and tell him we'll see 'bout that. Once we get to the horse barn, I hand him the brush and tell him to get busy. He works down one side of the horse while I pull the feedbag out of the corner cabinet.

"Pauline's here," he says.

"Where?" I ask.

"Upstairs talkin to ma and Lottie."

I go rushing outta the barn leaving Frankie to finish up with that horse brushing. Even clomping up the back steps two at a time I can hear women's voices trickling from inside. At the top step I smell fresh coffee perking and stop for a second to brush my hair back outta my eyes. I take a breath before I open the door.

Lottie and ma are setting at the kitchen table with Pauline between them. They're drinking coffee and finishing off slabs of yellow cake.

"Hey, Chet," Lottie says to me. "We got a visitor."

"Pauline," I says, ignoring Lottie. "It's real good to see ya."

"Take off yer shoes, Chester," my ma says when I step in from outside.

I don't wanna seem too contrary to my ma, so I rip off my shoes and drop 'em down onto the little rug next to the door

"Hi, Chet," Pauline says.

Pauline's got her blond hair stripped back into a pony's tail and her blue blouse matches her eyes and she's smiling wide at me, like I'm the reason she come the whole way here.

I fetch myself a cup of coffee from the stove and set down between Pauline and Lottie at the kitchen table. I watch Pauline's hands while she fiddles with the spoon in her coffee cup. My ma's bragging on the crumb cake she made today, telling Pauline she oughtta have another piece. Her and Lottie have a little back and forth about what kind of stuff is best to make pie crust when ya can't get no eggs. Pauline sets there distracted almost like she's waiting for a break in their talking. When my ma tries to remember something about wheat flour, Pauline looks at me and says that they ain't seen me round the tent camp for a while.

"My pa's been wonderin where ya been keepin yourself," she says. "He ain't seen ya on the picket lines."

I smile at Pauline.

"How is yer pa?" I ask.

Pauline says he's doing all right, getting one day a week up the Millionaire's Camp, which is a lumber camp on the other side of Ashtola.

"That lumbering is hard work, though," she says. "Worse than mining for sure. Short pay, pine trees crashing down all over the place like to crush a fella and the straw boss always giving you the evil eye to boot."

"I been workin some myself," I tell her.

"I can see that."

While Pauline looks round the kitchen at the wood table and coffee and tea on the counter and down the hall at the rug, Lottie says something else 'bout pie making but Pauline don't pay no attention. She says that I must be doing pretty good to have us living all fancy like this.

"What ya tryin to say, Pauline?" I ask her.

"Just that yer doin real good, Chet" she says.

At first I thought she was trying to pass some kind of judgment on me for working for Angelo, saying how we was living high on the hog and all, but there ain't nothing mean in her voice.

"So ya think it's okay what I'm doin?" I ask her.

"Ain't none a my business what yer doin."

I look round to make sure that Esther ain't nowhere in hearing before I start talking again. I sit up straight in my chair and talk to Pauline, but it's Lottie I'm looking at when I ask point blank whether or not she cares about me running liquor for them bootleggers.

"Heck, no," Pauline says.

"Way I hear tell, ya don't wanna have nothin to do with no bootleggers. Ain't that right, Lottie?"

Lottie's staring over at our ma like it's her job to get her outta this. But ma don't say a word, just goes over to the stove to get herself some more coffee.

"What I said to Lottie wasn't nothin 'bout no bootleggin at all."

When my ma comes back to the table, she spoons a heap of sugar into her coffee cup and clanks the spoon around mixing it up. She says to Lottie that she oughtta go see what Johnny's doing in the other room. Then my ma tells me and Pauline that she's gotta go and work on some of her afghan crocheting.

I'm fuming a bit at Lottie for causing a confusion, but Pauline being over at our place is a lot more important to me. Now that we're setting in the kitchen all by ourselfs though, I don't exactly know what to say.

"Ya got yer family doin pretty good, Chet," she says again.

"Thanks."

We set there for another minute looking round the kitchen at the cookstove and the canned peaches and pears and the aluminum cabinets fastened to the wall. I know it's gonna come out clumsy, but I figure I better ask Pauline what I wanna ask her before she starts to yawn and tells me that it's time for her to head home.

"Pauline," I choke. "Would ya wanna go out to eat with me some Saturday night?"

"I'd like that, Chet," she says. "That'd be real good."

Pauline's smiling and I'm smiling too when I tell her that I'll come get her down the Tent City in the horse wagon.

I says we'll go into Windber and get some restaurant food and then maybe, if she wants to, we'll go see the pictures at the Arcadia.

I ask Pauline if I can give her a ride back down 40, but she says that her pa's coming in from Ashtola and she's supposed to meet him down the train station to walk the tracks back to 40. I tell her that I'll see her on Saturday night. She says, "Goodnight, Chet." Standing in our doorway, she gives my hand a quick squeeze before she turns round to go. Once Pauline's walked off, I run my fingertips over where she squeezed my hand and it's almost like it's still warm.

After a quick run out to the barn to make sure Frankie done all right by Angelo's horse, I zip back up to the kitchen and set down at the table to have a piece of that crumb cake. While I'm setting there, Lottie comes out from the other room saying she's put Johnny to bed for the night. I tell her to sit down and she pulls out the chair that's across from me and drops her butt down on the corner.

"Chester," Lottie says. "Before ya say anythin, I want ya to know that I was just thinkin of you. I didn't wanna see you headed down the same road as Buzzy. I figured if you had to stop runnin with them damn bootleggers to get Pauline, it might be just enough."

I finish off the piece of cake I been chewing at while Lottie's talked. I says to her that it's fine that she's thinking 'bout me and all. It's good that she don't want to see me in no bad trouble. But she better not go pulling no kind of foolishness like that again, not if she wants to keep on staying on anyplace that I'm paying a rent. I don't let my voice go above talking, but I tell her if it weren't for me being mixed up with this damn bootlegging, Esther and Frankie sure wouldn't be in no school and Johnny wouldn't be getting no hot dinner every night.

We'd still be setting round with empty bellies trying to figure whether we're gonna starve to death or freeze solid before we get around to it.

It's a funny minute setting at the table after I say that. I'm getting ready to go on about how maybe she's my big sister and all, but I'm the one who's taking big risks running liquor across the county day and night. So at least I shouldn't be getting told no bullshit by my own family.

But when I look back up from my cake, I see that Lottie's crying a little. This is strange as hell cause I thought she'd be pinch-lipped and neck veins bulging, ready to push back herself from the table and start shouting, saying that she's near a grown woman and it's me that damn well oughtta be listening to her. But she just looks down into her cup and says she sorry.

"It's okay, Lottie," I tell her. "I ain't mad or nothing."

Lottie shakes her head and gets up from the table. After she brushes the corners of her eyes with her fingertips, she gathers up all the plates and the coffee cups and starts heating up a bucket of water to clean the dishes.

Nineteen

Friday, me and Sal tote the weekend liquor boxes up the stairs at Angelo's. The stairway's narrow and it's hard work trying not to clip each other with corners of them crates in the close going up and down, but still Sal's laughing, saying to me how much easier all this is going, working with me instead of Buzzy.

"No 'fence," he says. "But Angelo was always too nervous 'bout yer brother being wild to let him know what goes on here at the house. I had to do all the blend up my ownself and then drive every damn drop of this stuff up to the barber shop and have Buzzy load it up from there."

We pile that booze up in the back of the wagon in the cinder alley behind Angelo's and then draw the canvas over the top of the boxes. Sal dashes on a little bit of straw for good measure. He gotta ride the load the whole way down to Tire Hill to some rich fella who owns the slaughterhouse down there. Before I head back down into Angelo's cellar to finish watering down the rest of that bathtub liquor, I figure I might try to use Sal's good mood to see if he might know anything about what happened with Buzzy.

I remind him about the night the Pinkertons come for Buzzy, the way he came running down to Main Street to let him know they was looking.

"How'd them Pinkertons know to look for Buzzy in the first place?" I ask.

Sal ain't got one of them faces that can keep a secret, so I know he's telling me the truth when he says that he just come down to round up Buzzy cause Angelo told him to get off his ass and do it.

"Any more than that," he says, "ya gotta ask Angelo."

Washing off the old gin and vodka bottles is the first thing I like to do, so that way I ain't gotta fool with no rag when I'm done funneling that bootleg liquor. There's any spilled liquor, I just tell them hicks that a bottle must of broke rolling down from Canada.

"It's a long trip," I tell 'em.

I'm just finishing up the first case when Angelo comes bouncing down the cellar stairs. He's smoking the butt end of a dark brown cigar and blowing out little smoke rings into the air like he's in some kind a good mood.

"Pollock boy," he says to me. "I don't know what you do for fun. But you stay the hell away from them Sons a Itlee out Dunlo for a while."

"I don't never go there 'cept to take 'em liquor," I says.

"Don't take 'em nothin. They're gettin a visit from the cops."

"Shouldn't we ride out and let 'em know?"

"Let 'em know, hell!" Angelo laughs. "I'm the one who told the cops where to find 'em."

I guess them Dunlo fellas got behind in paying for their liquor or done something else to get Angelo on the warpath. He just says that the police gotta have somebody to haul off for pushing booze every couple months.

"They don't 'rest nobody," he says, "people says they ain't doin nothin 'bout all this liquor."

Angelo throws his hands up at them guilty cases stacked round his cellar and fetches hisself a glass of elderberry wine outta the jug on the table next to the door. He turns round and looks at me. I nod and he pours me a glass of wine too. I must look a little scared, cause he says that I don't have to worry. I know too much 'bout what goes on round here for him to ever think about handing me over to the police.

"I could stand to know a little more," I says to him. "When you sent Sal down into Windber to look for Buzzy the night he got shot down by McMullen. How'd them Pinkertons even know to look for Buzzy?" I ask. "One of them Eye-tailyan scabs give him up to the Cossacks?"

"Whatsa difference?" Angelo grunts.

He picks up the funnel and sets it down into the neck of one of the empty gin bottles. Then he flips up a gallon jug of bathtub by the little pig tail handle and starts pouring.

"I need to know, Angelo," I says.

"Whatcha worried I give yer brother to the cops for bein a pain in the ass?" he laughs. "Use yer head, Chet. If I'd a fixed it for yer brother to get hauled in, I sure as hell wouldn't a sent Sal down to warn him 'bout it. Nah, was a priest give him up. Heard Buzzy killed that scab in some confession," Angelo says.

"Priest?"

"The hunkie bastard what got moved outta here last month."

"At St. Cyril's?" I says. "Father Smelko?"

"That's the guy," Angelo says. "On the take from Berwind from way back. Old days."

When Angelo says this it's like something comes loose in my head, not like a wire, like a flood. Like a dam broke somewhere on the inside of my head, like water's rushing down, blasting away the meaning of everything like dynamite. My head's flopping from side to side. I feel like I might fall right

into the mixing table. My chin's on my chest and my stomach
twists like it's been flushed full of lye. I must look at the edge
of being like a mad dog. I feel my ass drop down onto a spare
crate. So much I don't want this to be true. So much.

Angelo looks over from pouring. He asks if I'm all
right. Balancing my hand on the crate, I stand up kinda shaky.
I tell him that I'm okay.

"I ain't had no supper yet," I tell him. "That wine went
straight to my head."

"You better not be into this liquor," he says.

"What happened to him?" I ask.

"Who?"

"The priest."

Angelo snorts.

"Bunch a miners went to see the bishop down
Johnstown. Told him if that priest kept preaching they should
give up the strike and get their asses back to work, they was
gonna light up the church for Christmas—with five gallons of
kerosene. Bishop sent him out to Ohio or someplace."

I nod real slow and grab up the next case of empty
liquor bottles and heave it up onto the mixing table. I can't let
Angelo get no kind of clue 'bout none of this. He finds out
I talked about a murder in confession or anyplace else, he'll
shoot me quick as look at me.

I drop the spare funnel down into the mouth of one
of them gin bottles and pick up a gallon jug of the Ashtola
bathtub. I hoist it up and start pouring, keeping my eyes on
that clear liquor draining down outta the funnel.

It's almost like I come to myself driving the horse
wagon. I'm way outta Dago Town, over on the East Side of
Windber, in the middle of Eighth Street. I can barely remember
Angelo stomping back upstairs or even filling up the rest of

them liquor bottles. It's just like all of a sudden I got the reins clutched in my hands and I'm creeping the horse wagon down past the rectory of the Polish church.

I haul back on the reins jerking the horse to stopped at the corner of Main Street. I climb down outta the wagon. Standing there under the gas lamps, staring at the sidewalk planks and the meat market hedges and the patchy brown grass running up from the sidewalk to the rectory and the church, I'm thinking about Buzzy zipping around that Ford, dodging McMullen's bullets.

It's almost like I can see him clear as moonshine, running up Eighth Street fast as the wind and then laid down dead on the brown grass with the blood leaking outta him and the breath already gone, he's flat on his belly and he's still. I can smell the gun powder filling the air thick as sulfur smoke off the bony piles and I can hear them Pinkertons laughing, joking about who's gonna pay for beer.

I shouldn't have never gone to that Hungarian priest. I know it. Standing here right where Buzzy fell, I'm getting to feel he was right about a whole bunch of stuff. That this whole world *is* rigged but good, and that's just fine for the Johnny Bulls and the operators, but if you're just some dumb pollock or dago that don't count for nothing—well, good luck.

I snatch up a chunk of splintered wood from the edge of one of the sidewalk planks. It's rough to my fingers and smells like creosote. I break off a strip 'bout the size of a stove lighting match and stuff it down into the pocket of my coat. Then I climb back up onto the buckboard and give the horse a slap with the reins.

When I get back to the rooms above Leone's, I come in quiet. The whole place is dark, and I can hear my ma snoring like an overstoked train. I pull my shirt off and hang it over the back of the chair and lay myself down with Frankie and Johnny on the mattress next to the window.

Frankie's woke up by the feather tick getting pulled off of him when I settle myself in. He asks where I been, and I just tell him I'm home now. I touch the top of his head, running my fingers through his hair quick, like petting a dog. I tell him that he oughtta roll hisself over and that he outta get some sleep.

Twenty

Saturday night, me and Pauline been setting in Muscatella's Restaurant for over an hour and I ain't said more than two words. Pauline's told me how her aunt's on the mend back in Allentown with her pa's family. She's told me about her pa cutting them pine logs up the Millionaire's Camp and how he got the two of them moved over to Cesri's boarding house after he earned a few bucks. She said about how messy them boarding house fellas is and talked about the way she's been cleaning and cooking over there to help out with the cost of them staying on.

I just been fidgetin on my chair, watching her lift that long spaghetti into her mouth or snap her teeth into them meatballs. Pauline asks me questions 'bout my ma and Lottie, 'bout the strike, 'bout living in Dago Town, but I mostly just keep staring down into my own plate of sausage and red gravy.

"Did I do somethin to make ya mad?" Pauline says finally. "Cause if yer just gonna set here and not say nuthin, I can walk myself back to the boarding house where they's pigs, but at least people talk to each other."

It counts for a damn lot, this dinner with Pauline going well, but I just can't seem to make anything to come out of my mouth. It's like all the words I've got are hibernating or maybe they're scared stiff that if they come mumbling out, somebody else will end up killed by the Pinkertons.

I'm looking round the dim light of Muscatella's, at the red and white tablecloths and all the men in their suits and women in their fancy dresses. They're chowing down on beef steaks and pork chops, but my stomach's fierce roiled and my mouth is plumb empty, no sausage and nothing to say.

"Ya didn't do nothin to make me mad, Pauline," I says finally.

We set there for another minute before Pauline asks if my tongue's out on strike. Truth told, I ain't got no idea what to say to Pauline or anybody else. I ain't said hardly a word to anybody since I learned the what's what from Angelo.

I shuffle the pieces of sausage round on my plate till Pauline finishes up her spaghetti. When she clatters her knife and fork down on the plate, I jump a little. I ask her if she wants 'em to bring her some coffee.

Pauline says she don't want no coffee. She frowns, asking me if I got bad nerves about tomorrow, it being the day that Charlie Dugan's due to come back to Windber.

"He's supposed to be bringin them newspaper men back from Philadelphia to write about the strike," she says. "My pa says the union's gonna have a whole bunch of men there at the train platform when they come in."

"That's what I hear," I lie.

"Yer gonna be there, ain't ya?"

"I dunno," I says.

Pauline's glaring at me, asking me what the hell do I mean saying, "I dunno."

"My pa said ya spoke up for us to stay on strike, Chet. That other men wanted to quit, but ya said we had to stick it out."

I understand what Pauline's trying to tell me, but it's hard to imagine men wanting to listen to a fella so stupid he give his own brother up to the Pinkertons.

"Pauline," I ask her. "Have ya ever had somethin happen that just takes the bones outta ya?"

Pauline softens up the way she's looking at me. She lets her hands drop down onto the tablecloth and lace together like she's praying. She pulls her top lip down into her mouth with her teeth. "When I was eleven, my mother got the influenza," she says. "Months after she passed, I felt like a dog wandering round hungry. Sniffing the ground all over the patchtown trying to catch the scent of people that long moved away."

My throat goes tight and my eyes fill up. I snatch my water glass and pull a quick sip into my throat, but it don't do no good.

"It's like that with your brother, ain't it?" she says.

I just sit there not moving, trying not to start up crying. Pauline moves her hands across the table so they're setting on top of mine.

"I'm sorry for sayin what I did 'bout Buzzy when I met you, Chester. I was mad as hell about what happened down the train station and looking for somebody to yell at that could hear what I had to say. I couldn't be that mad and remember Buzzy was a person that you loved, a person that was gone."

I just can't listen to this. I pull a fifty-cent piece outta my pocket and flop it down on the table. I tell Pauline that I'm sorry but I gotta go. I push myself back from the table and hoof it out of the restaurant onto Twelfth Street. I zip up the sidewalk in the cold and pull myself up into the wagon.

A minute later, Pauline comes marching out of Muscatella's and heads straight up the street. Grabbing hold of the buckboard, she hoists herself up onto the seat next to me and grabs hold of my hand. She pulls open my fingers and presses the change into my palm.

"Ya forgot this," she says.

I close my hand around the coins and shove 'em down into my pants pocket.

"It was me that got Buzzy kilt," I tell her.

She looks at me queer, like she knows I ain't making a joke, but can't quite figure what I'm saying either.

"How ya mean, Chet?" she asks.

I let my breath go and tell Pauline 'bout the whole business—the dago, the beating, how we didn't know them scabs was tricked into coming to 40. Then I tell her how I give Buzzy up in confession to the Hungarian priest.

"That's how they knew to come for Buzzy?"

I nod my head and we just sit still there in the wagon outside of Muscatella's. The air is icy and our breath is thick as smoke. Pauline shuffles herself over, pushing the weight of her body up against me.

"Ya can't blame yerself for what happened to Buzzy, Chet," she says. "Berwind havin that priest in his pocket, there's the real sin."

"I know it," I says.

And it's true, I ain't such a fool as not to be able to see that this patchtown life twists things till they ain't got no shape at all, but knowing it in my head ain't the same thing as being able to let it go.

"I don't know what to do, Pauline."

"Yes, you do, Chet. Ya need to get back on the picket line. Getting the union in here is the only thing gonna stop them Berwinds from doing whatever they want to us, turning us into whatever they want. Ya know that, don't ya?"

I nod and let go of Pauline's hands and take hold of the reins. I roll the wagon down 15th Street past the Big Office and the Arcadia Theatre where they're showing a picture called *The Immigrant*.

"I'm sorry 'bout this evening, Pauline," I says. "I'm sorry it was such a bust. I figured we'd have some kind of fancy dinner then go to the pictures and watch Charlie Chaplin."

"That woulda been real nice," she says.

Pauline smiles at me when I heave up the reins and we jerk to stopped at the door of Cesri's boarding house. She scoots over across the buckboard of the wagon and puts the palm of her hand down flat on my knee. When she slides her face in close to mine, my heart is racing like a mule trying to outrun a mine fire.

"Chet," she says real soft. "It was nice anyway."

Pauline touches her lips to mine. I let go of the reins and for a minute it's like all the stuff running round my head drops down into a deep shaft falling fast and quiet. Leaving me alone.

TWENTY-ONE

Thinking on it the next morning, tucked under the feather tick, I figure that Pauline's one hundred percent right. No matter what happened with that priest, or what them Cossacks done, I can't be missing Charlie bringing them reporters back to Windber. How am I gonna hold my head high as a miner, if I ain't there to tell them newspaper men how we been out on strike against damn Berwind?

I yank on my trousers and shoehorn my feet into my brogans, and I haul my *dupa* out into the cold down Somerset Avenue toward the Windber Station. The wind's funneling up Twelfth Street, swirling the coal dust into whirlwinds of soot. I'm putting one foot in front of the other and steeling myself up for them Cossacks, thinking about how they come in and trapped us down the 40 station when we stopped them from bringing in any more dago scabs.

But when I turn the corner outta the lee of the alley onto Twelfth Street, I can see this Windber Station picketing is a whole 'nother animal. First off, even though the locomotive ain't due for another hour, the whole railyard and Berwind Park back behind are both lousy with Pinkertons.

Them bastards are everywhere. Twirling their clubs and fiddling with their heavy pistols, they're shouldering miners off the sidewalks, poking at them, telling them where to stand

and shouting for them to move along, spitting tobacco at their boots. Pulling every kind of penny ante shit, them Cossacks are giving their damnedest to stir things up. It's like this time they been out and out ordered to get our boys riled to beat the band.

Folks gathered round the Windber Station seem different too. Where down 40 everybody was all like one bunch of miners, here it's like there's two whole *different* kinds of people what's grouped round watching out for this train.

Pushed close in to the platform, it's nothing but diehards clustered together down near the tracks. Booted out back in April or May, a lot of these fellas ain't been no place but on the picket lines for the last ten months. Their coats is thready and stained and ragged up round their bodies and their grimy caps is set cockeyed on their heads. With their hands in their pockets and puffing out steam, they're either pinched-lip quiet or grumbling mean. Staring east down the tracks, these strikers are dead serious. Everything they got is tied up with Charlie's train steaming down the tracks and them reporters telling the world the way we're getting robbed.

But a couple dozen yards back from the station, milling round the green and loafing on Main Street, the rest of the crowd don't look half so bad off. Some are the fellas that first took day work in lumber camps or men who been working more and more in the little mines towards Somerset since the weather started to go south. Others ain't even miners at all, just folks curious to get a look at Charlie Dugan or, more likely, them reporters.

Threading my way down through the crowd on the lookout for folks I know, I give a wave to Mikey and his pa over near the edge of the green by the white painted bandstand. They're shooting the breeze with Fatty Papinchak and a couple of the men what's left living in them company houses down 40.

I see Stash and Baldy too. They're leaning up against the wall of the Palace Hotel with the rest of the Eureka 37 crew. Ten in the morning, but every one of them look like they been in the liquor since before breakfast. Maybe it *was* breakfast. Their jackets is bulged out with bottles and tools, and they look ready to kick up dust at the drop of a hat. I don't even let on that I see 'em and just keep walking, moving closer to the platform.

I don't know whether it's the look of my new clothes or if maybe the time I been gone feels longer to them than to me, but when I get up into the crowd near the tracks most folks don't say nothing to me at all. And even the ones that do are looking down their noses, saying nothing but, "Howdy Stranger" and shit like that.

It ain't till I finally find Mr. Paul that anybody even looks really glad to see me. He's off to the side of the brick station building huddled with a couple motormen and some loaders from out Mine 35. He pumps my arm like he's drawing a five-gallon bucket of water and tells them fellas that we was over in the 40 Tent City together. They gimme the nod, but keep walking round trying to stay warm in their thin coats.

When I ask Mr. Paul what he thinks of all of this, he keeps his tone low and shakes his head.

"I don't like it one bit, Chet," he says. "Them guards is out for blood today. They know they can show them reporters some kind a riot and it's gonna be all over for us and some of these miners what come down here to raise hell, they still can't see they're just screwing theirselfs."

Mr. Paul says no matter what, he's glad I come down to the station. I tell him I'm glad I come down too, tell him that I really want to see Charlie coming back to Windber.

"I got to tell ya though," I says to him, "I'm glad this train's scheduled for morning. I can't be here all day. I got a delivery to make."

Mr. Paul nods a little uncomfortable and just says that we gotta do the things we gotta do. I nod back at him, but no matter what happens I had better be back at Angelo's by two o'clock. He's giving me twenty dollars for running out to Ashtola to pick up this week's load of bathtub from them shiners. I wanna be as good a union man, but I can't be giving the high hat to no twenty dollars.

When the train whistle sounds, we push forward, close to the tracks, so we're bunched up near where the train stops. The crowd is thick and there's a good many folks I guess, but it sure don't look like much if you was around for the big picketing we had going way back in April and May. Them early strike days, three times a week, three or four thousand men might come up to the Windber Patchtown mines from all over Somerset County. Every mine entrance they'd be shouting and yelling so loud you couldn't hear a stick of dynamite if it was blowing off your own britches. Signs would be flung up and men would raise hell something fierce, throwing eggs and pennies, vegetables, anything. Back April, we was really letting them Berwinds know that we was bringing the union into these Windber coal fields Hell or High Water.

Now, I don't know there's more than five hundred men even come out for the picketing and I don't see hardly no signs at all—just a couple of union organizers from up Cresson holding bed sheets that got "Welcome Back Charlie" and "OUT ON STRIKE" writ on them in barn paint.

Looking around through the crowd, I see something else that's funny. There ain't no police around. I don't mean Pinkertons or agency men, cause with Cossacks on every damn corner they're thicker than coal slurry. But running my eyes down Main Street and through the Miner's Park, I don't see none of the Windber police walking a beat nowhere. I don't even see a single Stater lurking round neither. It makes me nervous. Something ain't right here.

I try to say something to Mr. Paul, but when the locomotive screeches round the bend, the yelling starts up. Between all of the men chanting "UNION! UNION!" and the roar of the train, I can't get nothing across.

But when a dozen horse Cossacks come riding out of the 15th Street alley, we all get the picture right quick. High on them quarterhorses, the Cossacks force themselves between the folks hanging back and the strikers up close in near the tracks, trying to corral us just like they done down the 40 station.

Knowing better than to stick around this time, Mr. Paul shouts to the other fellas from 35 to get moving and grabs hold of my elbow pulling me along with him. We hammer our way through the thick of miners to the edge of the crowd where them horse Cossacks has formed up a wall.

Tall enough to see over most everybody's heads, Mr. Paul tells me how they're running everybody off behind us.

"They don't want nobody to see what's gonna happen here, Chet."

We try to push our way between the Cossacks, but they ain't having it. They stomp them horses forward, damn near on top of us, while the Cossacks further back drive their horses through the folks behind.

When the train doors open up, it's guards perched in every damn car. Only now, McMullen hisself is riding up at the first car. His face set harsh, he's leaning out from the steps waving his big pistol in the air and yelling for his agency men to get their shotguns trained on us.

"We're hemmed in here pretty good," I says to Mr. Paul.

Watching them Pinkertons sighting up their guns, he bends his mouth down close to my ear. He says, "You do what they tell ya, Chet. These bastards ain't foolin. They're looking to turn this into some kind a bloodbath."

Almost like he heard Mr. Paul, McMullen cracks a pistol shot into the air and we all turn to look at him standing like death in the doorway of the rail car.

"You damn pollocks was told to get outta here ten times already," he says to us. "Now yer all under arrest!" he yells.

Men are pissing and moaning, saying we ain't been told nothing and calling McMullen out as the sunafabitch he is, but nobody really does nothing, till one of them 37 boys lets a bottle fly up at the car McMullen's standing on. The bottle breaks with a little crash on the rail car maybe three feet below the window.

McMullen looks over at the wet spot on the car. He don't say a word, just shifts his pistol over, flicks the hammer back and fires a round off into the boy's hip.

The boy is screaming to beat all hell and Stash rushes over, trying to get some whiskey into the fella's throat before McMullen decides he oughtta shoot him again.

"Now ya see how it's gonna be," McMullen says.

He runs his eyes over the rest of us, but I don't think nobody's scheming about throwing nothing else, cause the only sound rising up through the trainyard is the screaming coming from the fella McMullen shot.

In the end it's maybe about two hundred of us they haul off to Somerset. I get separated from Mr. Paul and them fellas from 35 in the loadout and my *dupa* gets tossed into the back of a vegetable truck with some hunkies. Them Pinkertons run the whole lot of us south in a wagon train of trucks with deputy sedans full of Cossacks riding shotgun between.

By the time they get all of us unloaded out of them trucks it's near on dark. The Somerset Cossacks come storming out of the jailhouse puffing up their chests. They line us up like we're some kind a display they don't get in this neck of the woods too often.

"Don't look so tough to us," they says.

Them Somerset Pinkertons poke our freezing asses and guts with their shotgun muzzles, cursing us "damn shittin foreigners," and letting us know that we're gonna have to face a mean Somerset judge come morning.

While I'm getting marched to my cell I finally get a peek at a Windber cop I know, the fella what Sal gave the twenty dollars to back November. He's funneling coffee down his throat in the jailhouse lobby waiting on some sort a warrant. I twist my way outta the jail cell line and grab hold of the front of his police coat.

"I need some help," I says to him.

He curses me, saying that he can't help I was born a dumb pollock. Then he gives me a shove back into the line of union men headed for the cells. I'm grinding my teeth thinking that when I get outta here I'm gonna settle his bill and good. But when none of them Pinkerton guards is looking, he gives me the nod and ducks out the jailhouse door.

The Somerset Pinkertons shove me into a five-man cell that already got ten fellas in it so ain't nobody too damn pleased to get another body jammed in there. Them fellas are diehard Slovaks from out 42 and I don't know none of them too good. They're talking Slovak to each other and giving my clean clothes the evil eye, maybe thinking I'm one of the fellas been scabbing out Central City, so I don't say shit. I just lean my elbows against the bars and wait for Angelo to send somebody to bail my ass out.

Twenty-Two

It's damn near four o'clock the next afternoon when Sal gets out to the Somerset jailhouse with my bail. I ain't even been able to lie down in that cell, let alone get no kinda sleep, so I'm feeling right shot and smelling like a flower when the guards cut me loose.

"Angelo's plenty pissed at you," Sal says to me.

Dragging ass past the bars down the jailhouse hall, I just nod, trying to stay awake till I get to the wagon. Miners still locked up in their cells is staring at me walking out next to Sal. Some are whispering and some ain't so quiet, giving me a good earful of what they think of me for getting bailed outta the pokey by Sal Monteleone instead of waiting for the union lawyer like everybody else.

"Fellas come in from Pittsburgh last night to buy up that shine," Sal tells me.

"Uh-huh."

The sun's already down and the wind's blowing cold as hell when we get outside and climb into the wagon. It's starting to snow. I snap the collar of my coat up to try and keep my ears from freezing off. I tell Sal I'm beat all to hell, but he just shrugs and once we're out on the main road he tosses me the reins and sets to dozing off in the seat.

I know Angelo's gonna be fierce vexed 'bout me not

picking up that liquor, but it ain't like I done it on purpose. 'Sides there's more important things going on here than Ashtola moonshine.

"Hey, Sal," I give him a poke. "Ya know anything what happened with them reporters on the train? Did they see how we was hauled off?"

"Hell if I know," he says, half-asleep. "I was busy foolin with yer liquor."

I stick to the side of the road trying to figure what happened with them reporters when they seen us rounded up and trucked off to Somerset. Are they writing stories about how the Pinkertons run us in for nothing? Is it gonna be writ up in all the Philadelphia papers?

Figuring it's best to give Angelo a chance to cool down about that shine, I let the horse take its time the whole way through Jennerstown and across the length of Somerset ridge and back down the 160 hill into Windber. It's after seven o'clock when I roll up Tenth Street in front of the shop, but Anglelo's still fuming in that barber chair. The 'lectric bulb's shining down so I can see him gripping onto them red leather chair arms and looking daggers at me the whole way from the street.

"We're here." I dig Sal in the ribs. "I'm gonna put the wagon away."

Sal sits up and rubs his eyes. He tells me not to worry about the wagon. He says that I better get my ass into the shop and talk to Angelo. I says fine and jump down off the bench seat onto the sidewalk.

When I walk in, Angelo don't say a single word to me. He just hops down off of the barber chair and walks to the front door. He tugs down the shade and then turns round to face me. He steps up so close it's damn near like he's standing on top of me.

"I'm real sorry 'bout missin the shine pick up," I says.

Angelo still don't say a word or even open his mouth. He just brings his knee up right into my balls and *hard*. Nothing to it, I'm crumpled on the floor like newspaper.

He gives me two kicks with the heel of his shoe before I can even get a hand out to try and head off anything else coming my way. Tears are streaming down outta my eyes, and I tell him to stop, but he keeps layering them kicks on till all I can do is cry out high-pitched as a girl.

After I take seven or eight in my belly Angelo starts cross the room and I manage to get up to my knees. But I don't get no further 'fore he's back with the razor strap. He brings that leather swift and hard down onto me. I can feel it sliding into my skin, but it ain't even like pain for now. Just heat, almost like getting a burn from brushing against a cherried up coal stove.

I figure we're getting to the end of the whole thing when I look up to see him standing above me breathing heavy. But then he starts winding the strap round his fist, and I'm thinking that I'm about to catch a real beating now cause he ain't even gotta worry 'bout messing up his hand.

But Angelo flings hisself on top of me, pinning my arms to the barbershop floor. He gets that damn belt wrapped round my neck. His arms bulging, he rips it tight and starts choking the breath right outta me.

Grunting and coughing, I'm trying like hell to get my fingertips underneath that belt leather and for the first time I'm scared that he really means to kill me. I can't believe I'm about to get done in on the floor of some wop's barber shop over not getting twenty gallons of moonshine from some damn Ashtola hicks.

"You listen now!" Angelo finally says. "You listen to me, pollock boy!"

I'm glad when I hear this. I figure, anybody who's gonna get killed, nobody cares if they're listening or not. Ain't like they're gonna be around to remember what got said.

With Angelo's whole weight fixed on top of me and that belt so tight, I can't even shift myself to try and get away. He pushes in so close, ain't no smell at all but garlic and elderberry wine. Bending over me, he brushes his lips up against my ear and it's almost like I'm a girl he's messing with by force.

"No more union for you!" he says. "No more!"

I think he's gonna get up off of me, but he cuffs me cross the side of my face with the meat of his hand. Then he finally looses the belt up round my neck just enough so I can get a little breath.

"What I say?"

"No more union," I choke back.

I catch one more across the jaw before Angelo gets up off of me and sets hisself back down in the barber chair. He's sweating like a cold drink on a hot day and wheezing like he just run a mile. I'm swirling my tongue round my mouth checking for loose teeth.

Slumped a little, Angelo wipes down his face with a barber towel. He throws me a greasy smile and says that I'm a good worker and he really hated to do what he done. But, he says, I can't be getting no kind of special treatment round here.

"Anybody else, same thing," he says. "Maybe worse."

Still flat on my ass, I knead my fingers cross my neck trying to get my blood running. Angelo says again that he's serious, I can't be fooling with this union stuff no more. I'm working full time for him now. There's cash money at stake and this union cost me plenty already.

"I had to send cases a real whiskey to three Sons a Itlee last night," he says. "Cost ya seventy dollars."

"Me?" I says.

"Ya don't think it's right I'm gonna pay for you missin the pickup?"

I'm too busy feeling for broken ribs to even think about saying nothing. I just shake my head and try to keep my eyes turned to the floor. They're starting to tear up, but there's something else going on too. I'm feeling plenty hot about this whole business. I'm socking all of them feelings away to pull back out when they're gonna do me some good.

Setting up in that barber chair like dago royalty, Angelo says he'll give me a month to pay him back the seventy dollars. He'll just take it outta my pay, he laughs. Like the company store. Then he gives me a hand up off the floor. Standing close to me again, he smiles. He yanks a fold of skin at my cheek and gives me a quick, hard slap. He says I'm a good boy. All aches and bruises, I just keep my eyes to the floor, thinking how someday he's gonna get paid back for this beating and it ain't gonna be with no dollars.

On my way outta the shop, he says to me one last time that I'm working for him now and nobody else. I nod my head and push the door of the barber shop shut. I start down Tenth Street back to Leone's, but after a couple blocks I think better of it and head over towards Cesri's. I want to know if Mr. Paul made it back from Somerset with any news.

Walking along the edge of the plank sidewalk, it's damp and slick with a dusting of snow. I touch at them bruises purpling my ribs. This whole business is beginning to feel like one big icy sidewalk after chugging a half quart of Ashtola shine. No matter how careful I keep shuffling my feet, there ain't no way to keep my balance.

When Pauline opens up the door at Cesri's boarding house, she goes white looking at my face. She pulls me into their room asking if it was the Pinkertons or the jailhouse guards what done it to me. There ain't nothing I can say to this, so I just ask her where I can find her pa. I need to see him, I says.

"He ain't here," she says. "He come in real quick, but he went back out to see Charlie."

"Where is Charlie?"

"Ya don't know what happened to Charlie?"

Pauline fetches up a piece of cloth and splashes some water onto it. Frowning, she gives my face a hard swipe, smearing off a little of the dried-up blood. I pull myself away from her, letting her stand there with that rag.

"Pauline," I says.

She takes a step back toward the window, letting the rag go limp at her side. She opens her mouth wide and blows her breath out slow and down, like somebody who's tried hard as they can not to give up. She looks over at the paint peeling wall and I can tell she don't wanna say what she's got to tell me.

"Charlie's up the Miners' Hospital," she says. "He's hurt bad."

"Jesus," I says. "What happened?"

"I heard McMullen got to him somewhere on that train."

"What about them reporters?" I ask her. "How could McMullen get at Charlie with them reporters watching?"

"How should I know, Chet? You was closer than me."

Pauline and me look each other in the eye for a second. When she takes a step towards me, I reach out and pull her into my arms and lace my hands round the small of her back. Even with them bruises, her weight feels right against my chest and her white face is warm pressing in on my cheek.

Stepping back after a minute, I run my fingers down Pauline's arms till I'm just holding onto her hands. I squeeze her fingertips and run my thumbs cross the soft backs of her hands.

"I'm goin up to the Miners'," I tell her. "I'll send yer pa back."

I press a kiss onto Pauline's cheek before I turn to get outta that boarding house room. Not letting me go, Pauline keeps hold of me with one hand while she reaches up to trace a finger cross a belt cut on my face with her other hand. She smiles a little crooked at me and lets me go.

"Be careful," she says.

"I'm always careful," I lie.

I snap my coat collar back up over my ears and turn back around out the door. Tromping back down the stairs and out into the cold, I start hoofing it to the Miners' Hospital down the East End.

TWENTY-THREE

I recognize a couple of union fellas standing round the infirmary steps from that last union meeting up Gerula's. Cigarettes smoldered down to stubs in their thick hands, and eyes pegged to the street, these is the same heavy-shouldered, no nonsense fellas that rode with Charlie down from Cresson when men was grumbling about keeping on with the strike.

They must still be worried about the Pinkertons getting to him, cause they're shoulder to shoulder at the hospital door, and they ain't much on letting folks by. I guess they can see I ain't no phony police or else they're letting me slide on account of my face being all cut, cause I waltz right through 'em. I poke my nose into a whole mess of hospital rooms looking for Charlie, till I finally spot Mr. Paul sipping on a coffee down at the end of the hall.

"Mr. Paul," I shout. "Boy, I'm glad to see you."

Mr. Paul tries to shush me cause patients is out cold sleeping. But when I get closer and he sees my face is all cut up, he yanks me round the corner into the waiting room. Running his fingertips over them belt prints marking up my neck, he lets out a whistle.

"Them guards really gotcha," he says.

I keep quiet for a second trying to figure how to answer. But when Mr. Paul lifts up my chin for a closer look at them cuts, he can see in my eyes, weren't no guards done this.

I'm thinking he's gonna say something about how I deserve to catch it this way for working for them Black Handers in the first place. But he just clenches his teeth and plops down on the long plank bench.

"Where they got Charlie?" I ask him.

Shaking his head, Mr. Paul blows his nose on his sleeve a bit and points back to the ward room. I sidle down the hall and peek my head round the corner. Inside the room, I see Charlie laid out on the bed. Both his legs is coated up with plaster and hanging down from ceiling wires and his head's wrapped up so I can't see none of his hair. His eyes is sliding round and they're glassy as shooter marbles.

"Jesus Christ, Charlie," I says. "What happened to ya?"

"McMullen's boys broke his legs. Then the bastards cracked him cross his skull." Mr. Paul's followed me into Charlie's room. He drops his hand down onto my shoulder.

"What about them reporters?" I says. "Didn't they see how ya got beat? Didn't they watch us get rounded up?"

"There weren't no reporters on that train, Chet" Mr. Paul says.

"What?"

"I'm sorry, Chester," Charlie says soft. He sighs and his eyes slide off sideways to look at the fella next to him.

"They wouldn't come," Mr. Paul says to me.

"What ya mean they wouldn't come?"

"Berwind got a crew a stooges together. He sent them all down to Philly saying the strike was over," Charlie croaks out. "They made out like the strike already been settled and it was just a few bad apples still holding out."

I look from Charlie's busted skull over to Mr. Paul who's staring down at the tile floor. I stand there waiting for one of them to start saying how the union's gonna move on from what happened, but it's boneyard quiet in that room. Nobody's saying nothing. Not a damn word. I grab onto the sleeve of Mr. Paul's coat and ask him what we're gonna do.

"It's over, Chet," Mr. Paul says.

"Charlie," I says. "Tell him it ain't over!"

Charlie looks down to his hung-up legs and then over to the ward room wall. I'm watching his face close, but there ain't nothing coming. His lips is flat slack, and he just looks played out. Not a trick up his sleeve.

"There ain't nothin we can do, Chet," Mr. Paul says. "We give it our best."

"We'll get them operators next time," Charlie says.

"That's bullshit."

I wanna tell them not to give up, that we still got a chance, that we can't let them operators keep doing us dirt, but I don't know what to say. It's true a lot of men has gone back to the mines and I know the union ain't had no strike relief to hand out in months. If them sunafabitch reporters ain't coming to tell folks the truth about how Berwind's been robbing us, maybe Mr. Paul and Charlie's right.

I turn around outta the ward room and stomp out into the hall, plopping myself down onto the plank bench. I'm snuffling snot back into my nose when Mr. Paul sets down next to me.

"So we're just supposed to go right back to the way things was?" I ask him. "Just pretend this whole strike didn't even happen? That folks didn't die for nothin."

"I'm sorry things come out this way, Chester," Mr. Paul says.

He tells me how the union had to go in the hole just to bail everybody outta the Somerset jailhouse.

"With nothing more coming into the kitty," he says. "Nothing more we can do."

"Nothin we can do, my ass." I says. "What about McMullen? Maybe we can't get nowhere near them Berwinds. But we can make damn sure that bastard gets his due. Get him with the dynamite like folks was saying before."

"What's that gonna solve Chet?"

"Solve?" I says. "Who the hell cares what it's gonna solve? Ask my brother what it's gonna solve! Ask Charlie in there what it's gonna solve! Better," I says, "send a letter back to Allentown, ask yer own sister what it's gonna solve!"

I know damn well I crossed a fat line here and when Mr. Paul grabs hold of me and picks me up off the bench to whup me, I figure I deserve it. But my ribs send a pain streaking through me and I'm screaming to high heaven before he even gets one of them big fists anywhere near to my face.

Worry spreads quick across his gob and he lowers me back down on the plank bench and yanks up the cloth of my shirt. My ribs is plumped up good and shoe-size splashes of purple runs the whole way up to my armpits.

"Goddamn, Chet," he says. "Those don't look so good."

"I'll live," I tell him.

I tuck my shirt back down while Mr. Paul walks the floor next to me. Looking down at the tile, he says he can full well understand me wanting to fix McMullen for all he done, but he can't have no part of it. He says he ain't gonna be mixed up with no cold-blooded murder.

"Besides," Mr. Paul touches at the gash in my neck. "It looks to me like you got all the trouble you can handle without gettin tangled up with that bastard."

"So that's your answer to the next bunch of fellas McMullen goes after when they go out on strike?" I says.

I scoot myself up off the bench, button my coat up tight. I tell Mr. Paul I'll see him around.

Truth be told, my jaws is swelling up, my ribs hurt like hell and them razor strap slices ain't feeling so damn hot neither. But when I walk down the hall of that infirmary ward, I keep my head high and my back straight.

"Charlie," I says into the ward room. "Take care a yourself."

I'm still feeling plenty hot marching back down Main Street to Dago Town, but the further I go the more I'm feeling the wind slipping that cold air up under my coat. By the time I get up past Angelo's I'm mostly just straight tuckered. I got my throat wrapped up in my coat collar and I'm just putting one foot in front of the other. I didn't care for giving Mr. Paul the high hat after all he done for me, and he's right that I gotta get clean away from these Black Handers. But I just can't see backing down about McMullen neither. Maybe settling his hash ain't gonna change the whole world, but it's sure as shit the right thing to do in this here Patchtown.

TWENTY-FOUR

I must keep Frankie and them up half the night tossing the feather tick around and groaning about them rib bruises aching, but it gives me plenty of time to figure on how to get out of this mess. I try to weigh everything out like the tippleman throwing coal on that pit scale, not letting no one thing act like a foot on the tare to throw the whole calculating out of whack.

I know there's still gotta be a vote and all for ending the strike official like, but with the union stone broke and Charlie laid up, it ain't gonna be long in coming. Seems my part in this damn bootlegging had better come to an end right quick too. I gotta admit it's all right having all them folks tipping their hat when I come rolling up and saying, "Chester, this and Chester, that." But I'll be dammed before I pretend being some kind of bootlegging slave for Angelo Facianni and his Black Handers is a whole lot better than being a coal digging slave for EJ Berwind.

The next morning my jaw is swolled near to double and my throat looking like somebody tried to hang me but I got lucky and the rope broke, but I'm outta the house and ambling up Ninth Street before it's full light with a plan hatched. Rolling around with my ribs on fire I kept thinking about the night I asked Angelo about what happened to Buzzy and the way he warned me off of running with them Dunlo Sons of Italy cause he turned them in to the cops.

Far as I'm concerned, what's good for the goose is good for the gander and Angelo ain't the only one who can go giving somebody up to the police. Firsthand, I know them Staters are looking to put the bite on every bit of bootleg what's coming into Windber. I'm puffing up the steep curves of the Ninth Street hill watching for Coulson's dark sedan. I'm gonna put him wise to all the liquor mixing that's been playing out down in that greasy wop's basement. I'm sure he's lurking somewhere between Windber and the 160 crossroads, keeping his eyes peeled for bootleggers trying to slip wagonloads of shine cross the borough line.

Past the turnoff for the recreation park, on a steep downslope, his sedan sets half-hid behind some brambles. It ain't that hard to make out, cause all the leaves been off for months. I'm glad it's easy to find, cause all that walking has got my ribs feeling like they're spearing into my lungs. I slip off into the woods so I can creep up on through the underbrush on the passenger's side of his sedan away from the road. I don't want nobody getting a peek at the two of us talking together. Fooling with all this liquor night and day's made me awful cautious of the Pinkertons and the wops to boot.

"Hey, Coulson," I call to him from a stand of maples. "It's me, Chester Pistakowski. Ya throwed my family outta 40."

When Coulson springs out the door of his car, shiny forty-five pointing straight at me with the hammer drawed back and telling me to get my hands in the air, I come to realize that maybe this wasn't the best way to start off talking to him.

I keep my hands real high and far from my body, so he can see I ain't got no pistol while I'm yelling for him to put away that gun. I tell him I come up to these woods so to help his Stater ass out.

"What kind a help I need from a bootleg driver?" he says.

He starts to relax when he gets a good look at my swollen jaw. I take a step closer so he can see just how bad I caught it. I ask him if I can open-up my coat collar. I show off my neck, which is edging on toward blackberry. I also pull up my shirt to let him get a peek at them strap cuts and the bruising splayed cross my ribs, just so he sees I'm serious.

"So what's it to me that Angelo give ya a beatin?" Coulson says. His voice is sharp, but I can see he's surprised at how bad a whipping I done took. "I figure that comes with the territory for a smart ass like you."

"Cause this beatin," I tell him, "is gonna put a big feather in your cap."

We both climb back into Coulson's deputy sedan and with that cold morning air chilling me right through, I give Coulson everything I know about how Angelo runs that liquor— the moonshiners out Ashtola what's got the stills, the wops from Johnstown who slide the real Canadian stuff in from Pittsburgh, the room dug out under his basement where we water down the bathtub liquor and the names of most all the fellas who hand over the cash at the Sons of Italy and Slovak Halls. For good measure, I add Grubby Koshinsky's name to the list. When I'm done, even Coulson's ugly face has twisted itself to smiling.

We set there for a minute together in that car and he looks like a dog that got tossed the steak instead of the bone. But before he gets too used to knowing all this and decides he figured it out hisself, I says to him that he's gotta trade me one favor for me clueing him this way.

"Coulson, now," I says. "Only one thing you gotta do. You gotta make damn sure all of your Staters start their raiding down Angelo's basement first. He gotta be the first one you go rolling after."

"Whatza difference?"

"Cause every one of them other folks you're hauling to the pokey, you're gonna let them know it was Angelo what give 'em up and told ya how to find 'em so he could buy himself a lighter sentence."

Coulson damn near burns hisself with his cigarette, he's laughing so hard.

"Chester," he says. "If I knew what an operator you was before, I might not a been smiling so much when I seen you threatening two grown men with a sewin shears. You're a right shark."

"I can't say it was a goal," I tell him. "But it don't sound so bad neither."

I can still hear that Coulson chuckling when I slip back down over the hill into Windber. I got to tell Lottie to start getting our stuff packed up to go.

Back at the rooms above Leone's, Lottie gets her first daylight eyeful of how I'm looking and she's looking ready to pitch a fit.

"Chester," she whispers harsh. "I gotta talk to you."

I nod and let her grab hold of my sleeve, pulling me outta the kitchen onto the back steps, away from our ma and the twins. Standing out in the wind in her print dress, Lottie's saying she heard about what happened down at the train station. She starts in telling me that she knows I'm paying the bills and that means I'm running things round here and all, but she just can't stand to see me catch no more of these beatings. Coming from the Pinkertons or the Black Handers, she's right afraid the next one's gonna kill me.

"Just look at yerself, Chester," she says.

She pulls me over to look at my reflection in the kitchen window. She's near crying, staring at my puffed jaw and striped neck. She don't even know my ribs is anything but fine.

Taking my hand, she's pleading for us to use any money that I got stashed to get us the hell outta Windber and far away from all these Patchtowns too.

"You're right," I nod. "It's time for us Pistakowskis to make tracks."

Right to Lottie's stunned face I says there's no doubt about it, the powers that be are gonna have to be calling this strike off and soon.

"I wanna be clean away from here before they do," I says. "We been beat and the Berwinds ain't gonna let us forget it. With our best folks drove out or done in, they're gonna be making slaves of us worse than ever."

Lottie's smiling wide when I tell her she ought to start getting our stuff together, but don't be advertising it to nobody. I tell her to keep Johnny and the twins inside and let our ma know what's what when she's away from the neighbors, especially them dagos.

"Where ya goin?" Lottie asks, her voice falling. She keeps her eyes fixed on the horsebarn behind me, careful not to look no more at my raspberried face or throat.

I tell her that I ain't got no choice but to settle up some things before we go. Before Lottie steps back inside the door, she nods grim to me, thinking that I'm facing the long walk to tell Angelo that I'm quitting him.

"Be careful, Chester," she says.

Clattering down the stairs, I'm thinking things can't go on like this—all the women I know having nothing to say to me but, "Be careful."

TWENTY-FIVE

Wrapped up in Buzzy's old pea coat, I'm inching down the rails past the 40 powerhouse, my butt ducked behind the two tonners in the shadow of the high tipple. Since the sun come up, the wind is kicked up again and I can feel that air biting my face when I round the track bend outta the lee of the cars.

I keep my head low and stay near on my belly, sneaking down the tracks past the two guards in the rail car shop and stay low till I'm through the main yard. Once I get past the scales on the far side of the washhouse, out of sight of anybody looking out the window of the tippleman's shack, I do my best to make a sprint the whole way up to the other side of the works, near to the driftmouth where the tracks disappear into 40 mine.

My ribs vexing me, I peek out from the corner of the sand shanty next to the drift. I don't see nobody in the yard, just the line of yellow mantrip cars rusting empty on the tracks. After a deep breath, I crawl out on my hands and knees from the sand shanty towards the Little Office.

From low in the weeds, I can see McMullen through the Little Office window. He's setting with his feet up on the pit boss's desk smoking a cigar. Even leaning back, his body's all tense and he looks right ready to do a piece of mischief if a chance happens past. I can't see anybody else in the office, but all this bootlegging has made me plenty careful when fooling with the law.

I stay crouched in the thistle for a good ten minutes keeping my eye on the Little Office door. Sure enough, a couple laughing Pinkertons come stomping out. They stop dead in front of the sawmill to brag on how big a bonus they're gonna get from the Berwinds for breaking up our strike. With them bastards standing there, there ain't gonna be much chance for me to get anywhere near the powder shed to snatch up the dynamite or close enough to McMullen to lay it.

But remembering the way the snake didn't think nothing of shooting Buzzy down in the street, I ain't leaving outta this Patchtown without giving it my best to fix that wiry bastard. I fling myself across the passenger tracks quick as I can, diving into an island of high weeds between the Little Office and the powder shed to get them red sticks.

All this scurrying round ain't done my ribs one bit of good, so when I come down hard on a hefty chunk of bony, a loud grunt gets outta me and I gotta catch my breath for a minute.

On my knees, while that pain takes its course, I hear Mr. Paul's voice coming from outta the weeds ten feet off to my side.

"Chet," he says. "Keep yerself down."

Crouched so low my chest is scraping the top of the scrub grass, I scuttle towards him. Brushing them dry weed stalks between us to the side, I can see something in Mr. Paul's face is different. He could almost be somebody else, somebody I don't know. His mouth ain't got a whisper of smile at all and his eyes is flat black. It's like all the goodness been chased outta him.

"Whatcha doin here?" I says.

"Charlie." Mr. Paul shakes his head at me.

"When?"

"This mornin. That crack they splintered cross his head, it done him in."

"Don't think yer stoppin me," I tell him.

"I ain't here to hinder," Mr. Paul says to me.

Unfolding his big hand, Mr. Paul shows me a little pile of blasting caps and some hot wire. That's when I spy the fireboss satchel strapped cross his shoulder. With him in the lead, we crawl to the edge of where the weeds turn to coal dust up in front of the yellow brick Little Office.

Both of them guards is still loafing out in front. They're setting plunked down on the flat car smoking cigarettes. They ain't exactly vigilant, but it ain't like we can just walk right past them neither.

"What are we gonna do?" I ask him.

"Yer goin for a walk," he says.

"Ya ain't cuttin me outta this!"

"I wish I could, Chester," he says.

Mr. Paul opens the satchel and while he's fixing the hotwire to the dynamite pack he tells me to snatch up some bony chunks to heave at them guards.

"I want ya to skirt the long way round the powder house." Mr. Paul points back behind the drift. "And come up toward the Little Office from the other side along Paint Creek. No closer than one foot in the water when ya let them rocks fly," he says.

I remember the look on Buzzy's face the night I missed that dago way back when all this started. I don't want Mr. Paul booting me outta this plan, but I gotta be honest with him.

"I don't wanna let ya down," I says, "but I don't think there's a Chinaman's chance I can even hit them guards from that far off. Let alone do 'em any harm."

"Ya don't have to hit 'em, Chet," he smiles. "Yer just gettin 'em to chase ya."

I nod.

"Remember, only stay there till they start after ya. Then you haul yer ass across Paint Creek and over the hill fast as ya can."

"So I'm like the rabbit," I says. "They chase me while you plant that dynamite."

"I hate to say it. But that's about right."

"That's okay," I says. "I can live with that."

"Just run fast," Mr. Paul smiles stern, "or ya might not get to live with it for long."

One foot in the icy Paint Creek shallows, I'm panting like a summertime dog and my heart is racing powerdrill loud in my ears. I fix the first bony chunk in my throwing hand and sign a shaky cross before I start waving my arms and yelling at them Pinkertons.

"Hey!" I says, "Hey, ya Cossack bastards! Come get me, ya shitheels!"

Both of them Pinkertons haul their asses up off that railcar to peek down at me on the stream bank. They seem plenty griefed at me calling 'em out, but they're looking more lazy than mad. I let loose one of them bony pieces, but it lands way short and it don't look like they're going nowhere.

"C'mon, ya chickenshits." I start dancing up the hill through the railyard towards them. If they don't do no chasing, this here plan's dead as President McKinley. "Ain't younz got no balls to come take me on?"

Now they're just laughing cause they see I'm only a boy and maybe just looking to make a little mischief and they don't think I can do 'em any harm.

"Get outta here, kid," they says to me. "Before we settle yer hash."

The damn monkey looks on their faces swells me full up with so much hate that I don't even care no more what the plan was in the first place. I go running the rest of the way up the hill right for them, yelling and cursing like the devil.

"C'mon, ya fuckers!" I says.

I'm only maybe ten yards away and they're still laughing. I can feel the rage coming full on outta my heart, driving me closer in towards them. When I realize I'm also crying, I let one of them bony chunks fly.

It catches the nearer Pinkerton right in his fat face. Grunting, he raises up a hand and yanks it away covered with blood and I see the blood's pouring down outta his nose too. And that's that, them Cossacks is hot after me then.

I keep my stride high over them repair yard tracks, jumping rails and leaping from tie to tie. My footing's chancy in that shale, but I'm moving like the wind, gliding down over the hill outta the yard towards Paint Creek.

I can hear them Pinkertons' feet behind me crunching the cinders. They're carrying on and cursing me, but it don't mean nothing. I feel like I can outrun a buck deer this minute and I'm just counting steps till I'm knee deep into Paint Creek.

I hear 'em splashing slow into the orange water behind me and I'm wondering how far they're gonna go before they turn back, but I don't care. Let 'em run till they drop.

Once I get to the far bank, I turn around to get a peek at them winded guards before I head into the woods for the trail towards Windber. Water up to their ankles, both of them Cossacks is doubled over in the middle of Paint Creek with their hands on their knees. The one I clipped with that rock is smearing blood off of his face with the sleeve of his coat.

Glancing up past them wheezing Pinkertons, I see Mr. Paul making for the fan house at a dead run. His arms are pumping and his knees damn near catching his chest as he sprints away from the Little Office.

Putting my hand up like a salute to shield my face from the sun, I keep right on looking. I count, one, two, three and all of a sudden, there's a low rumble and them Little Office bricks is moving through the air like birds.

When they start to come down, I don't know, cause I'm long into the pine forest. My feet pressing deep in the soft needles, I'm putting acres of the thick tangle of evergreens between me and all of 40 Patchtown.

Twenty-Six

My last wagon ride outta Windber feels awful funny, like
it's halfway between the beginning of something and the end.
Lottie and the twins and Johnny are setting with my ma and our
heaped-up stuff in the back of the horse wagon we borrowed
from Angelo. Half dead after them Ashtola shiners cornered him
in a cell in the Somerset jailhouse, he ain't gonna be needing it.

Mr. Paul and Pauline is huddled up on the plank bench
next to me. I can feel the weight of Pauline's body pushed
up against my shoulder. Her touching me like that makes it
feel like maybe I won something here, even if a lot of things
been lost. Behind me, my ma's fiddling with her hands in her
lap, but she's smiling like I ain't seen her do since before the
strike started up. Her face easy, like she finally got her way,
Lottie's watching me and Pauline set next to each other on the
buckboard.

We're rolling up Ninth Street to the 160 T and from
there it's gonna be a long haul west. We're headed out for the
north Illinois fields where Mr. Paul says it's going on two years
that all the mines there are run full union.

Listening to the wood wheels clatter on the reddog as
we make the overlook bend, my mind's full up with all that's
happened. No small thing to be getting my family safe outta these
Patchtowns and to have cash money in my pocket. I'm flat tickled

that Mr. Paul's coming and even more that Pauline's coming too. But it ain't like coal and bony. No how I can separate any of this from us losing the strike or what we done to that dago behind McKluskeys or sure not what happened to Buzzy neither. I still got that creosote stinking splinter I yanked from the Polish Church sidewalk tucked away in the inside pocket of my pea coat.

How come we stuck so long after so many other people picked up and went? It's a fair question, no doubt. I could tell ya 'bout how 40 Patchtown was our home and we didn't want to give it up. Or I could say how once we started up the strike, we put so much of ourselves into it that giving in was the last, hardest thing we was prepared to do. Them things would all be straight true. But there's something else underneath all of that, or maybe shot all through it, like different colors of yarn in my ma's afghan crochet. It's just as much the truth as the other, but a damn sight harder to make clear for anybody else.

All I can say is that the Berwinds had so much say over what we done, telling us where to live, what to buy and when to work and when to sit home and starve, it was tough to see that anything was up to us at all. It's like the light from a carbide lamp in the middle of the day—ya can't even see it.

But I can see clear now. I'm looking down the hill to the lights of Windber and watching the smoke curl off the bony piles that jut into the sky between Dago Town and Eureka 32. I can see the whole way across the valley to the darkening fields on the other side. I'm leaving something here among these patchtowns, I know, but it seems to me I might be able to pick up something better if I lighten the load.

I lace one hand into Pauline's firm and I give the reins a little shake with the other. Listening to the horses clomp as we make the last turn onto the blacktop pavement of 160, I take a deep breath and smell that clear, cold air blowing in from the west.

ACKNOWLEDGEMENTS

If every individual who aided in bringing this book into the world were accorded proper credit, I'm afraid the acknowledgements would run longer than the text, but there are some folks whose contributions simply deserve recognition. At the very top of that list, alone, is my grandfather, Alex Valentine Dressick, whose kitchen table stories of men trying to bring the union into the coal fields in the 1920s are the reason this book exists. My grandmother, Margaret Swincinski, generously shared hours of conversation about farm life on the outskirts of the coal patch in the early part of the last century. I would also like to thank John Martino and Don Bertschman—not only for decades of friendship and encouragement, but also for reading and rereading this manuscript. Numerous folks also helped out with research and stories detailing coal town life, including Joseph and Joann Dressick, Walter and Julia Swincinski, and Tony Madoskey. Millie Beik's book *The Miners of Winder* and Phil Zorich at the library at Indiana University of Pennsylvania also proved to be of invaluable assistance. I would like to thank Larry Smith and the team at Bottom Dog Press for taking on this novel and their hard work to bring it out into the world. I would also like to thank Ann, without whom getting this and everything else together would have been near impossible. Lastly, and most importantly, I would like to thank my mother and father, Margaret A. and John F. Dressick for their support, not just during the writing of this book, but all the books that (thankfully) never saw the light of day. You guys were the best!

ABOUT THE AUTHOR

Born into a coal mining family in western Pennsylvania, Damian Dressick worked for many years as a marketing executive in New York, Los Angeles and Paris before packing up his kit to return to Somerset County to research and write the novel *40 Patchtown*. The book is inspired by an incident during the 1922 coal strike which his grandfather described while sitting around the kitchen table decades later. After renting a four-room wood frame "company house" in the coal patch town of Mine 37, Dressick spent months researching the rhythms of coal town life in the early part of the twentieth century, interviewing retired miners, their wives, and widows, and immersing himself in the coal heritage materials housed at the Indiana University of Pennsylvania.

Dressick drafted the novel in the duplex frame house, until an occupant on the other half set the house on fire in a failed attempt to murder his roommate. After being injured retrieving the manuscript from the house as it burned, the author revised the novel while living in Windber in the house of his maternal grandmother.

Dressick is the also the author of the story collection *Fables of the Deconstruction*. Winner of the Harriette Anrow Award and the Jesse Stuart Prize, his fiction and essays have appeared in more than fifty literary journals and anthologies, including W.W. Norton's *New Micro*, *Post Road*, failbetter.com, *Cutbank*, *Hobart*, *New Orleans Review*, *Smokelong Quarterly*, *Hippocampus*, and *New World Writing*. A Blue Mountain Residency Fellow, he holds an MFA from the University of Pittsburgh and a PhD in Creative Writing from the Center for Writers at the University of Southern Mississippi. Described by Frederick Barthelme as "an artist to be reckoned with," he currently teaches at Clarion University. Damian can be found online at www.damiandressick.com.

Books by Bottom Dog Press
Appalachian Writing Series

40 Patchtown: A Novel, Damian Dressick, 184 pgs, $18
Mama's Song, P. Shaun Neal, 238 pgs, $18
Fissures and Other Stories, by Timothy Dodd, 152 pgs, $18
Old Brown, by Craig Paulenich, 92 pgs, $16
A Wounded Snake: A Novel, by Joseph G. Anthony, 262 pgs, $18
Brown Bottle: A Novel, by Sheldon Lee Compton, 162 pgs, $18
A Small Room with Trouble on My Mind,
by Michael Henson, 164 pgs, $18
Drone String: Poems, by Sherry Cook Stanforth, 92 pgs, $16
Voices from the Appalachian Coalfields, by Mike and Ruth Yarrow,
Photos by Douglas Yarrow, 152 pgs, $17
Wanted: Good Family, by Joseph G. Anthony, 212 pgs, $18
Sky Under the Roof: Poems, by Hilda Downer, 126 pgs, $16
Green-Silver and Silent: Poems, by Marc Harshman, 90 pgs, $16
The Homegoing: A Novel, by Michael Olin-Hitt, 180 pgs, $18
*She Who Is Like a Mare: Poems of Mary Breckinridge
and the Frontier Nursing Service*, by Karen Kotrba, 96 pgs, $16
Smoke: Poems, by Jeanne Bryner, 96 pgs, $16
Broken Collar: A Novel, by Ron Mitchell, 234 pgs, $18
The Pattern Maker's Daughter: Poems,
by Sandee Gertz Umbach, 90 pgs, $16
The Free Farm: A Novel, by Larry Smith, 306 pgs, $18
Sinners of Sanction County: Stories,
by Charles Dodd White, 160 pgs, $17
Learning How: Stories, Yarns & Tales, by Richard Hague, $18
The Long River Home: A Novel, by Larry Smith,
230 pgs, cloth $22; paper $16
Eclipse: Stories, by Jeanne Bryner, 150 pgs, $16

Appalachian Writing Series Anthologies

Unbroken Circle: Stories of Cultural Diversity in the South,
Eds. Julia Watts and Larry Smith, 194 pgs, $18
Appalachia Now: Short Stories of Contemporary Appalachia,
Eds. Charles Dodd White and Larry Smith, 178 pgs, $18
Degrees of Elevation: Short Stories of Contemporary Appalachia,
Eds. Charles Dodd White and Page Seay, 186 pgs, $18

Free Shipping.
HTTP://SMITHDOCS.NET

CPSIA information can be obtained
at www.ICGtesting.com
Printed in the USA
FSHW012055210920
73967FS